COLORADO FREE REIN

BROTHERHOOD PROTECTORS COLORADO

BOOK TEN

ELLE JAMES

TWISTED PAGE INC

COLORADO FREE REIN

BROTHERHOOD PROTECTORS COLORADO
#10

New York Times & *USA Today*
Bestselling Author

ELLE JAMES

ISBN EBOOK: 978-1-62695-504-2

ISBN PRINT: 978-1-62695-505-9

To my fabulous editor for keeping up with me and making time when there is no time. Delilah Devlin not only rocks as an editor, she's a wonderful writer!
Elle James

AUTHOR'S NOTE

Enjoy other military books by Elle James

Visit ellejames.com for more titles and release dates
Join her newsletter at
https://ellejames.com/contact/

PROLOGUE

"Minz, cover me." Devin "Daredevil" Layne gripped his M4A1 rifle, bunching his muscles, ready for action. "I'll take point."

"I've got your six," Staff Sergeant Trace Minz said. "I'll be right behind you."

Twenty Green Berets of the 10th Special Forces from Fort Carson, Colorado, crouched in the shadowy ruins of buildings on the edge of a small Syrian town, awaiting the signal to move in.

They'd waited until night to infiltrate the town. Starlight shone down on them, lighting their way.

Intelligence sources from inside that village had identified a top ISIS leader responsible for the beheadings of a group of aid workers including doctors and nurses, sent in to help the civilians impacted by the shelling of several multifamily structures.

Their sources indicated their target Hajji al-Hassan would be surrounded by his guard and a couple of mercenaries the leader had engaged as his personal bodyguards. He'd hired one mercenary for himself and a female mercenary to guard his three wives, who were also located with him in a former government building at the center of the town.

The Special Operations Task Force had been given strict orders to find and neutralize al-Hassan. He was not to escape, even if it meant collateral damage to civilians who might be with him.

Devin didn't like it when terrorists used civilians as human shields. Though they'd been told to do whatever it took to take al-Hassan out, Devin would do his best not to kill women and children.

"Go," came the command from their team leader, Sergeant Major Mark Rutherford.

One by one, the men moved through the streets, entering the village at different locations, leap-frogging from shadow to shadow, covering for each other as they progressed toward the town's center.

On point, Devin led the team to their goal, the large government building at the town center. He came up from a side street at the west corner of their target with a view of the front of the building and the west side.

"Two guards at the west entrance," he whispered into his mic. "Two at the front entrance."

"Moving into position," Ace Monahan, their most

accomplished sniper, responded. He would take out the west side guards and then the front guards. Ace had a reputation for eliminating multiple targets before they could sound any alarm.

Using a silencer, he tagged the two guards on the west entrance, dropping them before either knew what was happening.

"Cease fire," their team lead ordered. "Motor vehicle coming up the street in front of the building."

A large, dark SUV stopped outside the main entrance. The driver, wearing loose black clothing and a black turban, got out. He leaned back into the SUV and pulled out an AK-47 rifle. After releasing the thirty-round magazine, he slammed it back into the weapon and rounded the vehicle, moving to the side closest to the front door. With his rifle at the ready, he stood with his shoulders back, his black-turbaned head held high and waited.

The SUV and its armed driver weren't part of the plan. So, what was an SUV doing there at that time of night? It was late, almost midnight.

Rutherford spoke softly, "Ace, be ready,"

"I can't get a clear shot with that SUV parked in front of the door," Ace reported.

Devin studied the building and the surrounding area. With the west entrance guards out of commission, the entire west side of the building was clear of ISIS rebels. "I can move closer," Devin said.

"Go," their team leader said.

The driver and the two guards turned as the double front doors opened. With the guards and driver preoccupied, Devin took the opportunity to move. Crouching low and keeping to the shadows, he raced for the west wall.

Three women dressed in black burkas were herded toward the SUV by a slim figure dressed in khaki pants and a khaki long-sleeved shirt. On her head, she wore a black hijab, which covered her hair and much of her face. She carried what appeared to be an AR-15 with a thirty-round magazine.

The female mercenary, Devin concluded. He hoped the women would move quickly into the SUV and leave the area clear for him to zero in on their target.

He dropped to his belly, doublechecked his rifle with the silencer fitted to the end and stretched across the ground.

Lying in the prone position, he brought his rifle up to his shoulder and stared down the sight, lining it up with the edge of the open front doors.

"Moving in behind you," Minz whispered into Devin's headset.

Moments later, Minz dropped to his haunches beside Devin. "The others are in position, ready to make this happen."

"Good," Devin responded. "We might need help."

All three burka-clad women settled inside the SUV, leaving the door wide open.

Their chauffeur was in no hurry to close the vehicle. Instead, he turned to the entrance and waited.

The female mercenary left the women and crossed to the building's main entrance.

Devin's gaze remained focused on that door while using his peripheral vision to scan the area for other movements.

The guards moved back a step as a squad of armed ISIS fighters exited the government building and spread out, weapons pointing outward, establishing a perimeter, and making Devin's job even harder. One fighter stood between him and the door. The man hefted his rifle to his shoulder and rolled his head from side to side as if working kinks out of his neck.

More movement at the door made Devin tense.

A black-bearded man dressed in khaki like the female mercenary, wearing a pair of mirrored sunglasses and a camouflage hat, stepped out of the building.

Behind him, a man in a long black caftan and a black turban stepped out, surrounded by a phalanx of men crowding through the doorway all at once. The man at the center of the clump sported a long, full white beard. Devin caught glimpses of him through the gaps between the ISIS soldiers, each carrying rifles. One man had in his possession a revolver-type grenade launcher. Another held an RPG over his shoulder. Those two weapons could mean a lot of trouble for Devin's team.

With all the men standing at the entrance, surrounding al-Hassan, Devin couldn't get a clear bead on their target.

"Fuck," Devin muttered and shifted his position, hoping it would help.

It didn't.

"Focus on the target," Rutherford said, his voice tense but encouraging. "He can't get into that SUV."

With the women tucked into the vehicle, only ISIS soldiers and the mercenaries stood in the way of Devin accomplishing his team's number one mission.

Take out al-Hassan.

His sights set on al-Hassan, Devin waited for a gap in the people milling about the entrance.

As the group moved toward the SUV, distance widened between the men surrounding al-Hassan. A gap opened.

Devin squeezed the trigger.

At the exact moment Devin committed to the shot, the female mercenary stepped between him and the ISIS leader.

Too late. The bullet was out of the barrel. A second later, the woman in khaki jerked and fell against al-Hassan.

Devin cursed. "Shit's about to hit the fan."

"Move in," Rutherford ordered the team.

Some of the ISIS soldiers scattered, and others

gathered around al-Hassan, moving him toward the SUV.

Devin aimed for the middle mass of the clump of bodies headed for the vehicle. Al-Hassan was not getting into that SUV.

He fired again, hitting one of the men in black, who was using his body as a shield to protect the ISIS leader. That man dropped, making the others stumble.

Minz leaped over Devin's prone form and knelt beside him, his rifle pressed to his shoulder. He fired into the clump, taking out another ISIS soldier.

Finally, Al-Hassan was in Devin's line of fire. He fired a round, hitting the man in the upper torso.

The ISIS leader jerked backward.

Devin fired again as the man swayed toward the SUV. The bullet hit the ISIS terrorist in the head. He crumpled to the ground and lay still.

"Daredevil and Minz fall back!" Rutherford said.

"Incoming!" Minz yelled.

Devin had only a split second to shift his gaze from the dead ISIS leader to the man in khakis who'd taken the RPG from the ISIS soldier and now held it over his shoulder, aimed directly at Devin and Minz.

Minz shoved Devin hard, sending him flying past the corner of the building. A moment later, the world exploded around them.

Pain ripped through Devin's leg, and shrapnel

peppered his body. His ears rang, and his head swam from the concussion.

Rifle fire raged around him as dust settled over his skin. Pain radiated up his leg and throughout his body. He looked around, realizing he'd fallen around the corner of the building. He remembered Minz pushing him.

His heart stopped for a frightening moment. Where was Minz?

"Minz!" he called out, his voice no more than a weak croak. "Minz!" In a haze, he tried to get up. His right leg didn't work. Every movement sent fiery pain ripping through his body, making him fade in and out of consciousness.

Devin fought to stay awake. Since he couldn't get up, he dragged himself across the ground to where Minz had been before the explosion.

What looked like a bloody lump of rags lay in a pile where Minz had been.

"Minz." Devin choked on his buddy's name as he gathered what remained of the man in his arms. "Goddamn it, Minz. You can't die on me."

His words went unheard. His friend was gone.

Tears spilled down Devin's cheeks as gunfire raged around him. His head swam, pain gripped him, and he grew weaker, finally succumbing to the black fog creeping in to claim him.

CHAPTER 1

"DEVIN LAYNE? Or should I call you Daredevil?"

At the sound of the voice behind him, Devin turned, a frown forming on his forehead. Daredevil was a moniker he no longer attributed to himself. Not since his last deployment—the mission that had taken the lives of some of his best buddies in the 10th Special Forces and had gotten him a one-way ticket out of the military. He flexed his aching leg and faced a man with black hair, black eyes, and a military haircut. "I'm Devin."

The man stuck out his hand. "Jake Cogburn. My colleague, Max Thornton, asked me to talk with you."

Max Thornton? Devin remembered Max Thornton. He'd been a member of the 10th Special Forces a couple of years before Devin. Max had been on a mission with him sometime in the past. Then Devin hadn't heard or seen anything about Thorn—the call-sign he'd gone by—for several months. "So? Am I supposed to be impressed?"

Jake gave him a quick grin. "No. But he said you were a top-notch Green Beret."

"Past tense," Devin said, turning away. "If you'll excuse me, I'm working."

"I know. I don't want to take up too much of your time here. But I'd like to buy you a drink and talk."

Devin shook his head. "I'm busy."

"How about tomorrow…Gunny's Watering Hole…seven o'clock?" Jake persisted.

Irritated, Devin gathered his horse's reins. "Like I said, I'm busy."

"At least, think about it. I have a job opportunity you might be interested in." Jake touched his arm. "Just hear me out over drinks. I think you could be an asset to our organization."

Devin snorted. "I doubt it." He stood for a moment by the fence overlooking the arena where the Fool's Gold, Colorado, annual Gold Rush Rodeo was taking place. This was the first job he'd landed since he'd come home to Colorado, and it was only for the duration of the rodeo.

Yeah, he had some money coming in from his medical retirement from the Army, but his dissatisfaction wasn't so much with the money as the need to work. The problem was there weren't too many opportunities for a man who could barely get around. Unless he settled for a desk job. He frowned.

"How did you know I'd be here?" No one except his immediate family knew he'd returned to Fool's Gold.

"I ran into your sister, Laurel, in town." Jake Cogburn leaned his elbows on the rail, watching as a contestant lowered himself onto a huge bull in the chute.

Seconds later, the gate opened, and the bull leaped out. The man held on to the rope around the bull's middle for four seconds before the frenzied beast threw him.

"Laurel has a big mouth," Devin muttered.

"Laurel cares about her brother," Jake countered. "Besides, I asked about you. She didn't want to lie, so she told me you'd come home."

"So, I'm home." Devin shot a narrow-eyed glance at Jake. "How did Thorn know to ask about me?"

Jake gave a hint of a smile. "He has connections in the Special Forces like I do from my time in the Navy SEALs. We belong to an organization called the Brotherhood Protectors. We recruit former military, who are highly trained for Special Operations, and put them to work."

Devin's frown deepened. "Look, I don't know what Thorn thinks, but I'm not the same guy who fought with him in Afghanistan." He took a step away from Jake, demonstrating the decided limp. "I didn't quit the Army; they processed me out because of this." He patted his leg.

Jake lifted the leg of his jeans, displaying a prosthetic. "I get it. This civilian life is new to you, and you're trying to figure out how you fit." He shook his head. "I was where you are not long ago until an old buddy of mine, Hank Patterson, pulled my ass out of the bottle I was trying to drown myself in and gave me purpose. I didn't think I could be useful to anyone when I was one leg short of a pair." He lifted his chin. "Hank proved me wrong. And I'm here to offer you the same deal he offered me. Come to work for the Brotherhood Protectors. We need men like you."

Devin wanted to believe what Jake was saying, but it all sounded too good to be true. "I don't need anyone's pity or handouts."

"We aren't handing out either. You have to work for your pay on our team. Some of our assignments are dangerous. But, tell you what, don't say no right now. Think about it. I'll be waiting for you tomorrow at the Watering Hole. I'll buy you a drink."

"I have to get to work," Devin said.

"You don't have to commit to anything." Jake held out both hands, palms up. "What can it hurt?" He grinned. "See you tomorrow." And he left.

As soon as Mallory Watts drove up to the arena, her horse trailer in tow, she could sense something was different. She'd been to the Fool's Gold arena so many times in the past twenty years, she could find her way around blindfolded. Hell, she'd cut her teeth riding barrels and had fallen in love with a bronc rider.

But that was another story she'd just as soon forget. That bronc rider had chosen to join the military. On one trip home on leave, he'd promised to come back and marry her the next time he came home.

She snorted in a very unladylike way as she parked the truck, climbed down, and strode to the back of the trailer. Jazz pawed the floor of the trailer, more anxious than usual.

"I get it," Mal soothed. "I feel it, too." She unlocked the gate, swung it open, and stepped inside. After untying Jazz's lead, Mal backed her out onto the hardpacked dirt. "Let's just do what we came to do and go home to a warm stall and a bucket of sweet feed, all right?" She rubbed the horse's muzzle and patted her neck.

Jazz tossed her head as if ready to do her part and get back to the Lucky Star Ranch.

Mal's edgy feeling didn't go away and must have transferred to Jazz because the animal tugged against the lead and danced sideways.

"Whoa, girl," Mal whispered. "We have to wait our turn." She glanced over the top of her horse's neck at a man on a horse, wearing the polo shirt of one of the arena's security staff. His hair was a rich brown, cut short on the sides and barely longer on top. The guy sat straight in his saddle, his hips swaying with the horse's steady gait as if he'd been born to ride.

A memory tugged at Mal's heart. If she didn't know better, she'd think it was…

No. It couldn't be. She'd know if he was back. Surely, he would've called her if he was coming home. At the very least, Devin would've called his sister Laurel to tell her he was home. And Laurel was her friend. A friend would tell her friend when a certain former fiancé was in town.

Mal shook her head.

She moved around her horse to get a better look at the man. Her pulse kicked up a notch, and her breathing grew erratic. If she weren't one of the most down-to-earth women she knew, she'd think her mind was playing tricks on her.

Then again, Devin had been gone far too long. His sister had mentioned he'd been injured and was in rehab at Walter Reed Hospital in Maryland. When Mal had asked for details, Laurel had insisted Devin hadn't wanted any visitors. Still, she'd gone out to Maryland anyway, only to be turned away. The man *really* hadn't wanted visitors. Not even her.

That had hurt. A lot. And she hadn't heard from Devin for several months. It was as if he'd fallen off the face of the earth. Had he lost interest in her? Was he blowing her off?

"Mal!" a voice called out, pulling her back to the

task at hand. Laurel Layne hurried toward her. "Whew. I'm glad I caught you."

Mal's eyebrows drew together. "Hey, I didn't think rodeos were your thing now that you have your own florist shop?"

Laurel beamed at her. "When my bestie is riding, and it's in town, I'm there. Besides, I have a good helper now. She's manning the store today. And isn't it a glorious day to be outside and riding?"

"It's okay, I guess." Was it her imagination, or was Laurel overly upbeat? Mal glanced back toward the man on the horse, wishing her friend had waited a few more minutes to find her. Surely, the guy would've turned his head just enough to reveal he wasn't Devin, and she'd have gone on to do her ride free of curiosity. Distractions made her lose focus. If she didn't have focus, she'd lose the race. She'd been training hard with Jazz. She deserved her attention and commitment after all she'd put up with.

"I've been meaning to call you," Laurel said.

A flash of guilt tugged at Mal's gut. Laurel was always the one to call or keep in touch until about a week ago. "No worries. I've been busy out at the ranch. We got a new quarter horse to train. I've been working it steadily for the past few days, and I figured you were busy with the shop."

"Yeah," Laurel glanced away. "We've been busy, but I meant to call and let you know—"

"Stay tuned, folks," an announcement blared out. "Next up is the barrel racing competition. You don't want to miss this event. You might want to empty what's full and fill what's empty before the fun begins."

Mal's head shot up. "That's my cue. I'd better check in before they think I'm a no-show."

"But Mal—"

"Can we talk after my ride?" Mal asked as she slipped the bridle over Jazz's head and buckled it in place.

"It might be too late by then," Laurel muttered so low Mal wondered if she'd heard her correctly.

Mal reached for the saddle horn and looked over her shoulder. "What did you say?"

Laurel gave her a weak smile. "Nothing. You go do your race and show them how it's done. I'll be here when you get back."

Mal nodded, her frown deepening. "Is there something you wanted to say?"

Laurel shook her head. "Nothing that can't wait. I know how you like to focus. So, get in your zone, or whatever, and we'll talk when you've won the race." She winked and stepped back.

Mal swung up into the saddle, still frowning. Laurel was acting weird. However, Mal didn't have time to figure out why. "We'll talk after," she said and rode toward the staging area to wait her turn.

As she stood in line behind the other riders, she glanced around.

No sign of the man on the horse.

Good. She could focus on the race ahead. Mal leaned over and scratched behind Jazz's ears.

The first barrel rider came in at just over twenty-one seconds.

Mal gave the woman a nod as she rode out of the arena. Good, but not great. She and Jazz averaged closer to eighteen seconds. Nineteen on a slow day, and seventeen and some change on good days.

The next rider burst into the arena.

Movement from the corner of Mal's eye drew her attention away from her competition. The security guy in the polo shirt rode into full view around the corner of the concession stand.

Mal's heart leaped into her throat and pounded hard inside her chest. Joy filled her, sending a rush of warmth to every part of her body.

It was Devin. He was home. Sweet Jesus.

A smile spread wide across her face. Without thinking about it, she nudged Jazz and turned her toward the man who'd held her heart in his hand from the moment they'd met at this very arena fourteen years ago. Granted, Devin took a little longer coming to the same conclusion. But when he'd come back on leave after a deployment, they'd reconnected.

No sooner had the horse started toward him then a thought edged its way through her euphoric haze. How could he have a job as arena security the day he got back? Unless he'd been back for several days, maybe longer. If he'd been back for more than a day, why the hell hadn't he contacted her? And why had he insisted he didn't want her to come out to Maryland after he'd been injured? Isn't that what fiancées did for their true loves?

A thousand questions rushed through her head. She pulled back on the reins, a frown pressing her eyebrows together.

At that moment, Devin glanced her way. His gaze met hers, and his eyes flared. But like a flame blown out, they grew shadowed, and he looked away.

"Oh no, you don't," Mal muttered under her breath. She pressed her booted heels into Jazz's sides, urging the horse forward.

When Devin turned his horse away, Mal sent Jazz into a trot, catching up before he could get away.

"How long have you been back?" she demanded.

He refused to meet her gaze again. "What does it matter?"

"What does it matter?" She sputtered, anger building deep inside and bubbling to the surface like lava about to spew. "I haven't heard from you in months. You refused to let me come to Maryland when you were injured, and then you show up at a rodeo in our hometown as if nothing is wrong."

Devin's lips pressed into a thin line. "Nothing *is* wrong."

"The hell, you say." Mal was just getting revved up. "What happened to talking with the woman you promised to marry? You cut me off without any idea of what's going on. You didn't even let your family in on your condition, your prognosis. All they knew was that you were alive and back in the States. At least *they* got word. *I* got nothing."

"I didn't want to bother you," he said.

"Didn't want to bother me?" Mal's anger turned cold. "Well, it didn't work. I was bothered. I went to Bethesda to find out what was going on. They wouldn't let me in to see you. They said you had specifically told them no visitors, even family."

"I didn't want anyone there," he said.

"Why? Did you ever think that people who love you could've helped with your recovery?"

He shook his head. "No. There was nothing you or anyone else could do to help."

"Why?"

"I'm not the same man who left Fool's Gold."

Mal's gaze swept over him. "You look like the same man."

"Looks are deceiving." For a brief second, his gaze met hers. A shadow crossed his face, but then he looked away. "I've changed."

Her breath caught and held in her throat. "Or is it that you've changed your mind about us?"

"Fine," he said, his voice harsh. "Yes. I've changed my mind about us. There is no us. There. Now, will you leave me alone?"

The rodeo announcer chose that moment to say,

"Next in the arena is Miss Mallory Watts, a five-time winner of this event, here in this arena. Hold onto your hats, ladies and gentlemen, she's fast!"

Mal stared into Devin's eyes, hurt pulling so hard on her heart she could barely breathe.

"You're up." Devin tipped his head toward the arena gate. "You better hurry before you forfeit."

And that was it. He'd dumped her.

Mal lifted her chin, spun her horse around, and entered the starting gate.

The gate flew open, Jazz leaped out, and the race was on.

Moisture filled her eyes, making it hard for her to see the barrels. She made it around the first one, thanks to Jazz and the hours of training. When they rounded the second one, she was completely blinded by tears flowing down her cheeks. Her knee clipped the barrel, knocking it over and giving her an automatic five-second penalty. Jazz skittered sideways and kept going. Somehow, they completed the event and raced out of the arena.

Jazz stopped twenty yards past the gate, no thanks to Mal. The reins hung in her hands, and the tears streamed down her cheeks, dripping off her chin. Yes, she'd known something was wrong with her relationship but had held out hope that Devin would come back to her and make it right. She loved him with all her heart.

Her broken heart...

"Mal," Laurel's voice broke through her misery. Her friend, the sister of the man who'd just dumped her, touched her boot. "I'm so sorry," she said. "I tried to warn you, but…" She sighed. "I'm sorry."

"We're through," Mal whispered, and more tears slipped down her cheeks. She'd never felt this empty in her entire life. She sat on her horse, unable to function, barely able to breathe.

"He's not the same," Laurel tried to explain. "He's angry at the world. I've never seen him this way."

"He's not the same?" Mal flung her hand in the air. "What does that mean? He's Devin, for God's sake."

"His injury…" Laurel looked past her.

Mal turned to see Devin on his horse, looking their way. "He never let me in to see him when he was in Bethesda. It hurt then. But this…" She looked away from Devin, afraid he'd see the tears he'd inspired.

"Damn him," Mal said through her teeth. "Why did he have to come back at all?"

"He had nowhere else to go," Laurel said.

Mal brushed the moisture from her cheeks. "He can go back to his beloved Army for all I care."

Laurel shook her head. "He can't. They medically discharged him based on his injury. He's without a job for the first time in his adult life."

And he hadn't bothered to let her in on any of his pain, his status…his freakin' life! He really was done with her.

"Tell me the truth, Laurel," Mal pinned her friend with her stare, "did he fall in love with his nurse during his stay at Walter Reed?"

Laurel shook her head. "No way. He's only ever loved you."

Mal fought back more tears, swiping away those that came anyway. "I call bullshit."

"You have to give him time. He's trying to process his life without the military. He seems kind of…" Laurel raised her shoulders and let them drop, "lost. Like he has no purpose, no direction."

"He had enough direction to tell me to leave him alone."

Laurel snorted. "If it makes you feel any better, he's told everyone who loves him to leave him alone."

Everyone? Mal turned again.

Devin was in the exact same spot, still seated in his saddle, looking toward her, a haggard expression on his face.

Something tugged at her heart.

No. She wouldn't feel sorry for the man. He'd done the dumping, not her.

Still…he did appear like Laurel said…lost.

Her instinct was to turn Jazz around and confront Devin, calling him out for dumping her. What injury could be so bad that he'd be kicked out of the Army? And what could be so bad that he'd push away all those who loved him?

He appeared to be the same Devin who'd left

nearly a year ago, promising to come back and marry her after his deployment.

Well, almost like the same Devin. Those shadows beneath his eyes and the gray tinge to his skin weren't normal.

Three boys ran past her, laughing and playing tag. One of them raised his hand in the air, holding something in his fingertips. He laughed and slammed his hand down. A sharp pop sounded like a hand-held firecracker.

Jazz reared.

It was all Mal could do to keep the horse from landing on the kid. She pulled hard on his reins while trying to stay in the saddle.

When the horse came back down on all four hooves, she took off, the bit between her teeth, and ran like the wind.

No amount of hauling back on the reins or shouting *whoa* got through to Jazz. She was scared and was getting away from the noise that had spooked her.

And she was heading straight for the busy highway that fed tourists into Fool's Gold at sixty miles per hour.

Mal had to get her to stop before she reached the road, or she and Jazz would become roadkill or cause a massive and deadly pileup.

CHAPTER 2

DEVIN HAD WATCHED as Mal ran her race. It was as if she didn't give a damn or couldn't see what was in front of her. When she'd blown out of the arena, he'd been on the verge of swallowing his pride, riding up to Mal, and telling her he'd been wrong and didn't want her to leave him alone. She was the last person he wanted to leave him alone.

He'd just nudged his mount forward when a kid set off a firecracker beside Mal's horse.

Jazz reared up on her hind legs.

Devin sucked in a sharp breath.

As experienced as Mal was, the surprise of a horse, rearing like that, unseated even the best riders.

Mal held on, struggling to bring the animal down without taking out the culprit who had been stupid enough to set off fireworks near the horses.

When the horse dropped down, Devin almost

breathed a sigh, but Jazz wasn't done. She took off with Mal on her back, racing faster than he'd seen the animal move in the arena. Hell, if she didn't slow down, she'd make the highway in less time than it took to run a barrel race. Horses and speeding vehicles didn't mix well.

Devin slapped his mount's hindquarters with the reins and raced after Mal and Jazz.

They were well ahead of him and widening the distance.

He dug his heels into his gelding's flanks and leaned forward in his saddle. The only saving grace was that Mal was leaning back on her reins, pulling hard enough to slow the animal. Unfortunately, it appeared Jazz had the bit between her teeth. No matter how hard Mal pulled, she wouldn't stop her.

With his heart in his throat, Devin pushed forward, gaining on the runaway horse. They were within fifty yards of the highway when he finally caught up. With his horse abreast of Jazz's, he edged closer, reached out, snagged Mal around the waist, and pulled her out of her saddle and onto his lap.

The frightened animal kept going.

Mal refused to let go of Jazz's reins and almost yanked herself and Devin out of his saddle.

Devin dug his boot heels into the stirrups and pulled hard on his horse's reins.

Mal held on to Jazz's reins, turning her as Devin slowed his mount.

A few short yards from the highway, the horses halted.

Winded, Jazz heaved air in and out of her lungs. Lather covered her chest and neck, and she foamed at the mouth.

Mal struggled in Devin's arms. "Let go of me."

"I can't." Devin tightened his hold to keep her from falling to the ground.

But Mal wiggled so much that Devin was losing his grip. "If I let go, you'll fall," he warned.

"I don't care," she said. "Let go."

He didn't have a choice. Mal slipped from his grip and fell to the ground at the horses' feet.

Jazz reared again and would've run out onto the highway, but Mal hung onto her reins even though she lay flat on her back. The horse dragged Mal with her.

Devin dropped down from his horse before remembering his leg wasn't strong enough to hold his weight on impact with the hardpacked dirt. He fell to his knees and groaned as pain shot up his leg. He fought to rise, managing only by holding onto his gelding's stirrup. When he was finally up, he hurried to where Mal was being dragged toward the highway, shouting, "Whoa!" to her spooked horse.

Limping heavily, he managed a shuffling run. He caught up, snagged the reins and brought the horse and the woman to a halt.

Then he dropped to his knees beside Mal,

grimacing at the pain it caused. "Oh, sweetie, are you all right?"

"I'm fine, except for the scrapes across my backside." Mal stared at him, at the leg he was favoring, and then up into his eyes. "Is this why you're pushing people away?"

He frowned, his back stiffening. "I'd rather not talk about it." He pushed to his feet, fighting hard not to show how much it hurt to straighten.

When he reached down to offer his hand, she stared at it, her eyes narrowing.

"I call bullshit," she whispered as she laid her hand in his.

When he brought her to her feet, she didn't let go of his hand. Instead, she held on tightly and pressed her chest to his.

The warmth of her hand and her body flooded through Devin. After the explosion, when the medics had carried him into the chopper and airlifted him to the field hospital, all he'd thought about was this woman and how much he wanted to hold her again.

The surgeon at the field hospital had told him he was lucky to be alive with as much blood as he'd lost. He'd told the doc he had a girl back home he wanted to see, joking that he'd had to get blown up for the chance to go home.

When it was all said and done, and the doctors at Walter Reed had looked at the damage caused, they'd said he'd be medically discharged. That's when it had hit home. He was jobless, with no skills other than he was a good shot and had great skills in a battle. How useful would that be in the civilian world?

As useless as lipstick on a pig, as his father would've said if he were still alive. No. He couldn't go back to Fool's Gold and expect Mal to marry a man without a job and no prospects.

Mal wrapped her arms around his neck. "Did you hear me?" She raised her eyebrows. "I call bullshit."

"I don't know what you mean," he said, his voice hoarse, the effort of remaining stiff and remote straining his control. He was exactly where he'd wanted to be. "You deserve more."

"More what?" she challenged.

"More of a man," he said, his tone gruff with anger at himself, his shortcomings, the situation...hell. Angry at his life.

"So, you get to make all the decisions in this relationship? I don't get a say?" She laced her fingers at the back of his neck. "Tell me that you don't feel anything for me. That you don't love me, and I'll walk away."

Devin's anger bubbled up. He gripped her hips, his fingers digging into her soft flesh. "Damn it, Mal."

"Say it," she demanded.

He stared down at her, fully intending to tell her that he didn't love her, but when he opened his mouth, he said, "I never stopped loving you."

Then his arms came up around her, and he

crushed her to his chest. "Thinking about holding you in my arms was the only thing that got me through that first night, the surgeries and the torture of physical therapy."

She cupped his cheek in her hand, her eyes filling with tears. "Then why didn't you let me come to you?"

His jaw hardened. "I didn't want or need your pity. I didn't want you stuck with a washed-up guy who was only half a man. You deserve more."

"Again, are you the only one making decisions in this relationship? There are two of us." She leaned up on her toes and brushed her lips across his. "I choose you."

"But I'm not *me* anymore," he insisted. "I'm not fit to fight. I'm not good behind a desk. I used to know exactly what I wanted to do in life and had a plan for how I'd get there. Now, I don't know who I am."

She held his face between her hands, forcing him to look into her eyes. "You're Devin Layne. The man I fell in love with at this rodeo fourteen years ago."

He stared into her beautiful gray-blue eyes, and his heart melted all over again. He loved this woman with all his heart.

"You're worthy, and you're strong. You wouldn't have made it this far if you weren't," she said.

Recalling the grueling pace at which he'd pushed himself to learn to walk again on his damaged leg, he couldn't deny her words. A lesser man would've given up. Even when he'd wanted to quit, he'd pushed through the pain, knowing he had to get back to Colorado to see Mal, even if he couldn't be with her.

God, she was strong, beautiful and everything he'd ever wanted. He was tempted beyond anything he'd ever experienced to step back into their relationship and hope for the best.

He stared down at her, his heart pounding hard inside his chest.

"No. I can't do this to you. I don't know where I'm going or what I can do outside of what I was trained for in the Army. It's not fair to you to have to drag me along when you're able-bodied and capable of so much more." He set her at arm's length, though to do so cost him every ounce of control he had left. "I have to get back to work, even if it's only for the duration of the rodeo."

She frowned. "What about us? Are you calling off our engagement?"

"Can't you see?" He released her arms and shoved a hand through his hair. "I'm freeing you."

"Devin Layne, you are the most stubborn man I've ever had the misfortune to meet." She lifted her chin, her nostrils flaring. "This is the first time since I've known you that you've just given up. I never took you as a quitter."

Her words hit him square in the chest. He tamped down his knee-jerk desire to lash out. "Yeah, well, I've changed. Goodbye, Mal." Before he lost control, he spun and nearly fell flat on his face when his leg didn't fully cooperate. Devin stumbled, righted himself and walked away, his cheeks burning almost as much as his heart.

Mal was the best thing that had ever happened to him. She'd just told him to his face that she still loved him and wanted to be with him, even if he wasn't the same man he'd been before the explosion.

If he were a selfish man, he'd take her love and be with her. It's what he'd wanted most from the day they'd met.

He'd also wanted to join the Army and do his part to protect his country like his father before him, and his father's father before him.

The military was ingrained in his family. A tradition, he refused to break. He'd wanted to get established before he brought anyone else into his life on active duty. And he was where he'd wanted to be as a member of the elite Green Berets, ready to take on the world. That's when he'd asked Mal to marry him.

Now, with the military behind him, what did he have left? Not a damned thing.

His hands tightened into fists. He couldn't do that to Mal. He wanted the best for her—and the best wasn't him.

. . .

As she watched the man she loved walk away, Mal's heart squeezed so hard in her chest, she could barely breathe.

"Mal!" Laurel rushed to Mal's side, pressing a hand to her chest. "I was up in the stands when I saw your horse, with you on it, racing toward the highway. I couldn't get out of the arena fast enough. Not that I could have done anything to stop Jazz." She drew in a shaky breath and let it out. "Whew. Thank God, you're all right."

Then she looked into Mal's face and frowned. "You're not all right, are you?"

Her gaze following Devin's retreat, Mal shook her head, those damned tears slipping from the corners of her eyes. She angrily brushed them away, disgusted at herself for shedding another tear for that man.

Laurel glanced over Mal's shoulder, her frown deepening. "Oh." She faced Mal. "I take it you two had words."

Mal nodded. "It's over." She brushed past Laurel, gathered Jazz's reins and trudged toward her horse trailer. As she passed Laurel, she said, "Your brother called off our engagement. He says it's for my own good. I deserve better. Blah, blah, blah."

Laurel snorted and fell in step with Mal. "That's bullshit."

Mal's lips tipped upward for a moment. "I called bullshit, too."

Laurel shook her head. "You're the best thing that ever happened to Devin, and he knows it."

Mal stopped at the back of her trailer. "Oh, he didn't argue about that. He argued that I deserved better. Do you mind?" She handed Laurel Jazz's reins.

"Not at all." Laurel took the horse's reins and reached up to stroke the mare's nose. "My brother is an idiot," she cooed to the horse. "Isn't that so?" She stroked the animal's nose again and then turned to Mal. "So, what are you going to do about it?"

Mal opened the heavy door of the trailer and swung it wide. "I don't know. I need time to process all of this."

Laurel grimaced. "You're not going to hate me, are you? For not telling you he was back in town."

Mal frowned. "I should be mad. You're more than a friend. You're the sister I never had."

Laurel's shoulders sagged. "I feel the same. And I really wanted to tell you sooner, but…"

Mal touched her friend's arm. "It's okay. It wouldn't have made our first meeting any better had I known."

Laurel's lips twisted into a wry grin. "Yeah, but you might have done better at your event."

Mal shook her head. "With Devin here, knowing he wants nothing to do with me, I doubt I'd have done any better."

Laurel flung her arms around Mal. "I'm so sorry."

She stepped back. "But, deep in my heart, I know it will all work out. Just give him time."

"You're ever the optimist, aren't you?" Mal forced a smile. "I'll be all right. It was just a shock seeing him for the first time in months." Her heart constricted in her chest, and her eyes burned. She turned to her horse so that Laurel didn't see just how *not* all right she was.

Mal slipped the bridle off Jazz and snapped a lead onto her halter. When she had her tears in check, she turned around, tied the lead to the trailer and flipped the stirrup over the saddle. "What about you?" she asked to defect the attention from her own sorry excuse for a love life. "I heard you were seen with a new guy in town. Anything else you want to tell me?" Mal cocked an eyebrow and stared over Jazz's back at Laurel.

Laurel's cheeks filled with a pretty pink color. She shrugged, though a smile quirked the corners of her lips. "Yeah. I met the new guy in town at Mattie's Diner."

"Give me all the deets," Mal encouraged.

Laurel's eyes lit up. "His name is Alan Croft. He moved to town a week ago for the crisp mountain air. He's about the same height as Devin, has green eyes and black hair with a touch of gray at the temples."

Mal tilted her head to the side. "Just how old is this guy?"

Laurel laughed. "He's thirty-six. The gray is hereditary. His father had the same gray at the temples from the time he turned thirty-five."

Mal laughed. "You asked?"

Laurel's brow wrinkled. "Well, yes. I wanted to know everything about him."

"And he told you everything?" Mal loosened the strap through the girth and pulled the saddle off Jazz's back. "Most importantly, is he married?"

Laurel shook her head. "He's widowed. His wife died not long ago. Thus, the move to the mountains. He wanted a fresh start free of reminders of her."

"Oh, sweetie," Mal shook her head. "You do not want to get involved with the man. You'd be a rebound affair. They never last. At least that's what I'd always heard."

Laurel's lips twisted. "I know. That's why I'm going slow. If nothing else, it's nice to have someone to go to dinner with."

"How many times have you gone out with this guy?" Mal carried the saddle into the trailer and hung it on the saddle tree. "And where have I been that I didn't know all this?"

Laurel laughed like a giddy teen. "I was busy at the shop, and you're always busy with the horses at the ranch…"

"There's this cool new-fangled device people use for communication called a phone." Mal came out of the trailer, her hands fisted on her hips.

Laurel shrugged again. "I don't know...it's all too new. I met him at the diner a week ago. We went to the casino for dinner one night, and I have a date with him again tonight. We're going to the Springs for a movie."

Mal frowned. "Are you sure that's a good idea? I mean, you barely know the guy. He could get you in his car, drive off and never come back. Have you had a background check run on him?"

"Mal, don't be silly." Laurel's lips pressed into a tight line. "He's a nice guy."

"So was Jeffrey Dahmer," Mal pointed out.

"Well, he's not Jeffrey Dahmer," Laurel said. "And we're only going to a movie."

"How would he feel if you made it a double date?" Mal untied Jazz's lead and walked her into the trailer.

"I'm sure he'd be fine with it. Why?" Laurel stood at the door to the trailer, her eyes narrowing. "Are you suggesting that you'd come with us?"

Mal nodded. "I don't have anything pressing tonight. I could do it."

Laurel crossed her arms over her chest. "And your date would be...?"

Mal ran her hand the length of Jazz's back as she walked out of the trailer to join Laurel. "I don't know. But I'm sure I could find someone."

Laurel's lip curved up on one side. "Do you want me to ask Devin?"

Mal jerked back. "No way." Inside her stomach,

butterflies erupted in a swarm. She pressed a hand to her flat belly and lifted her chin. "I'll find someone else."

"On such short notice?" Laurel shook her head. "You've shot down every man in the county while Devin's been gone. They've all moved on."

Mal swung the door shut. "Surely, not all of them are gone. Don't worry. I'll find someone."

"Seriously, I can get Devin to come," Laurel said. "You don't have to call it a date. Just two friends joining me and my date for a movie."

"Does he even know you're going to Colorado Springs with this stranger?"

Laurel rolled her eyes. "Sweetie, I've been doing my own thing, without my brother's permission, for years. I'm not going to change how I run my life just because he's in town."

"Good point." Mal sighed. "Let me find my own guy to go to the movie. It's too soon for me to be in the same vehicle with Devin."

Laurel gave her a gentle smile. "You're right. That would be hard. And, if you do find another guy, maybe it will make my thick-headed brother come to his senses about ending things with you."

Mal lifted her chin. "It would serve him right if I found someone else and got on with my life."

"Damn right," Laurel said. "You've waited long enough. It's time for you to live. You're not getting any younger, and that biological clock must be ticking pretty loudly by now."

Mal's eyes widened. "You did *not* just say that." She snorted. "You're older than me. I have plenty of time left." She poked her finger at Laurel. "Ha! You're the one feeling your biological clock ticking. Is that what this is all about? Are you looking for Mr. Right so you can settle down and have children?"

Laurel blushed a bright pink. "No. I didn't say that."

Mal crossed her arms over her chest. "But you're feeling it, aren't you?"

Laurel shrugged one shoulder. "Now that my business is well-established and I have an assistant who can run it in my absence, the thought of having a family has crossed my mind. I don't want to wait until it's too late to have children. I've always wanted kids." Laurel sighed. "I've just been too busy after my short stint in the Army and then coming back home to start my life over."

Mal draped an arm over her friend's shoulder. "You had a rough time of it on active duty. You weren't in a good place for a relationship when you came back from Afghanistan."

Laurel nodded, her brow furrowing as if remembering that bad place she'd been. "I couldn't have found a better job back then."

"Martha took you in like the daughter she'd always wanted." Mal smiled. "From the wilted mess you were when you came back, working with Martha had you blossoming into your old happy self."

Laurel smiled. "Martha was an angel. The job I took when all I wanted to do was crawl under a rock and melt into the hillside ended up surrounding me with beauty and happiness. Now, I'm living my best life."

"Martha was glad to have the help. She'd gotten to where she struggled with the arrangements. Her hands were so gnarled with arthritis, she wouldn't have stayed open as long as she had, if it hadn't been for you." Mal glanced down at her own work-roughened hands, wondering how long she'd be able to work with horses.

Laurel looked off into the distance, a sad smile on her face. "I wouldn't be where I am today if not for her. I wouldn't be where I am today emotionally as well as career-wise. When she died, I thought I would die, too. She really was my surrogate mother."

"She must have known you'd need purpose when she passed on," Mal said.

"If not for the flower shop, I might've backslid into depression. I still pinch myself. We weren't even related, and she still left me the shop."

"And you've expanded it into the back where she used to live, making it even bigger and better. She would've been so proud of you."

"I hope so." Laurel smiled, her eyes glassy with

unshed tears. "She was my guardian angel, then and now." She sighed. "I miss her."

"Me, too. Hell, anyone who knew Martha misses her. She was a special soul."

"She made every floral arrangement with love." Laurel's gaze met Mal's. "Look at us, getting all morose when the sun is shining, and we have our whole lives ahead of us."

Mal closed the trailer door, marveling at how quickly Laurel could turn a somber mood into joy. "When you find Mr. Right, are you going to move out of the shop's upstairs apartment?"

Laurel sighed. "Probably. I want a yard where I can plant flowers."

Mal secured the latch and brushed her hands across her jeans. "And where your children can run and play."

"And maybe a dog." Laurel laughed. "I'd better not mention any of this to Alan. Most men would run screaming from a woman with marriage, babies and settling down on her mind."

"I think they like to think it's their idea." Mal looked away as her heart pinched hard in her chest, again.

"I'm sorry," Laurel said. "Here we are talking about marriage and babies and you—" She clapped a hand over her mouth.

"And I'm destined to remain single, childless and without a partner to grow old with." When Laurel opened her mouth to protest, Mal raised a hand. "Don't give me your optimistic prediction. I prefer to wallow in my misery for a little while. At least grant me that."

With a tight frown and a quick dip of her chin, Laurel acquiesced. "Okay, but don't wallow for more than a few days. You have a full life to live, with or without my stupid brother."

Mal didn't bother to point out that Laurel had once again injected her optimism into Mal's crappy day. Why bring the florist down when everything was sunshine and happiness in her friend's world? Business was booming, and she had a new guy to date. No one was pissing on her daffodils.

Never mind Mal's world had just crumbled to the ground like a dated Las Vegas hotel, heavily laden with explosives, imploding within.

Okay, that might be laying it on thick, but they were her thoughts, her broken heart and she was allowed a morose moment or two, damn it!

CHAPTER 3

He should never have come back to Fool's Gold. His return only reminded him of everything he'd lost, hammering the fact home that his life had changed forever. And not for the better.

After his encounter with Mal, he'd ridden off, determined to fulfill his duty of providing security for the rodeo.

While watching for recalcitrant kids armed with firecrackers, he couldn't help that his gaze returned often to where Mal had parked her trailer. He had to force himself to turn the other way so many times, he decided to return to the parking area on the pretext of looking for anyone doing things they shouldn't be doing.

When he got there, Mal and her trailer were gone.

The emptiness that hit his gut threatened to overwhelm him. If he hadn't been astride a horse, he would've crumpled to the ground. Several deep breaths and a pathetic excuse for a pep talk later, he moved on, determined to put the past and Mal behind him.

He couldn't let second thoughts cloud his judgment. Mal was the same strong, healthy, beautiful woman she'd been when he'd left her, promising to come back and marry her. He'd imagined ultimately returning to Fool's Gold and revitalizing the small ranch his parents had left to him and Laurel. Laurel hadn't been interested in ranching or living in the house they'd grown up in. Like him, she'd been forever changed by her time in the Army. She didn't like being isolated. She preferred life in town, close to other people and her business. Devin had dreamed of going home, raising some cows, horses and children.

With a bum leg, he wasn't fit to run a ranch, wrangle cattle or even get down on the ground and play with his own children.

Hell, he didn't even have a job to support a family. Thankfully, he didn't owe money on the ranch and house his parents had left him. He'd offered to buy Laurel's half, but she'd refused her share, insisting he keep it all. She had the flower shop Martha had left her in her will. When she wanted a house, she'd pay for it out of the money she made.

Devin had money set aside from his time in service. Money he would give Laurel when she did decide to purchase a house. In the meantime, he needed a job to help fund the improvements he planned to make to the ranch house and the ranch itself.

After his one-day job as rodeo security, he knew he had to find more permanent employment.

The next evening, after working all day in the ranch house, painting walls, he showered, shaved and dressed in his best black jeans and a button-down shirt. Against his better judgment, he drove to Gunny's Watering Hole to meet with Jake Cogburn. The least he could do was to listen to what Jake had to say. Having a drink with the man didn't mean he would commit to working with the Brotherhood Protectors.

Even though he resisted the idea that he could be of use, he was intrigued by Jake. If a one-legged man could make it work...

Devin pulled into the parking lot and parked his truck between two other ranch trucks and eased out of the driver's seat onto the ground.

The pain in his leg was a lot less than when he'd started physical therapy, but it was still there. He'd weaned himself off the pain medication, aware of how easy it was to become addicted. He'd seen the effects of pain medication addiction while he'd been at Walter Reed Military Medical Center in Bethesda, Maryland. Already handicapped by his injury, he refused to be even more of a burden on his family and society than he already was.

His goal was to work his way back into the best physical shape possible. The doctors had said he might not ever walk on that leg again. He'd proved them wrong.

Now, he only had to prove to himself he was still a viable human male, capable of taking care of himself and anyone else who might come along.

If he could get to that point, he might be able to stand beside Mal as her partner, not her burden.

If that meant eating his words and listening to what Cogburn had to say, so be it.

Doing his best to walk without a limp, he strode toward the rustic building made of corrugated tin and pushed through the doorway.

Once inside, he glanced around the room filled with a few women and mostly men. None of them were Jake Cogburn.

He checked his watch. He might be lame, but he was rarely late. Just as he suspected, he was right on time.

He looked around again.

A wash of relief swept over him at the same time a sense of failure knotted his gut. Jake was a no-show. The slim chance of a potential job slid into no chance. Devin was back to square one. Unemployed and crippled.

He started to turn toward the exit when a cute

female bartender with sandy-blond hair waved. She looked like someone he ought to know. Someone who had hung around Laurel when she was a teen. If he remembered correctly, she went by her initials.

"Devin Layne," she called out.

He turned back.

The woman beckoned him toward the bar.

He crossed the floor, reluctance and his sore leg making his progress slower than it should have been.

As he neared, the blonde grinned. "You're a sight for sore eyes. Been a day or two since you've been around. I bet Laurel and Mallory are glad you're home."

Laurel, maybe. Mal? A definite no.

He gave her a chin lift as her initials came back to him. "RJ. It's good to see you. Actually, I'm surprised you're still here. I would've thought you'd leave as soon as you were old enough." Most of the kids he and Laurel had grown up with had left Fool's Gold for careers in the bigger cities.

RJ shook her head. "This is home. No place I'd rather be—except maybe soaking my feet in a hot tub." She grinned. "Jake's in the kitchen. He said to tell you he'll be right out after he makes a couple of sandwiches. Gunny had to run back to the lodge. One of the guests tried to flush a baby diaper down the toilet." She grimaced. "Just another day at the Lost Valley Lodge. Have a seat, and let me pour you a drink."

"I can't believe Gunny's still working both the lodge and the bar," Devin said. "I'd have thought he'd be retired by now."

"Gunny retire?" RJ laughed. "He'd tell you he *is* retired—from the Marine Corps. We all swear he lives by the philosophy of he can sleep when he's dead." She swiped a rag across the counter. "Name your poison."

"Whiskey neat." Devin slid onto a bar stool, thankful for a little alcoholic fortitude to make it through this meeting.

Seconds later, RJ had a glass of amber liquid in front of him. "Hungry? Jake makes a mean bacon cheeseburger."

"No, thanks." He'd eaten a couple of slices of day-old pizza before he'd left his house. It sat like heavy shoe leather at the bottom of his stomach.

"Jake should only be a few more minutes. He would've been out here, but it got busy and then the clog at the lodge…" She shrugged.

"So, does Jake work the Watering Hole as well as what he does with the Brotherhood Protectors?" That didn't bode well if he had to work two jobs to make ends meet.

RJ nodded. "Yes, and no. As part of the deal to rent out the lodge's basement for the Colorado division of the Brotherhood Protectors, Jake agreed that when his team members don't have a current assignment, they help at the lodge and on the Lost Valley

Ranch. It's helped us out tremendously and gives the guys a sense of purpose when they're in between assignments."

"What if they have other obligations at their own places?" Devin asked. "Surely their families like them home."

RJ nodded. "It's really more voluntary than anything, but the guys like helping out." She nodded toward a broad-shouldered man with black hair and blue eyes, heading toward them with a tray-load of empty bottles and mugs. "Take Cage Weaver; he's between assignments. He and his fiancée, Emily, the redhead waiting on that table full of cowboys, help out quite often."

Devin studied the man. "He's one of Jake's team?"

RJ nodded. "But let Jake tell you about the team. He knows their backgrounds better than I do."

"Whose background?" a voice said behind Devin.

Jake pushed through a swinging door, carrying a tray filled with hamburgers and French fries. "Give me a second to get these to some hungry cowboys before they start a fight." He winked and crossed the floor to the table where the redheaded female was gathering empty bottles and mugs.

The man RJ had identified as Cage Weaver set his tray on the counter. "We need a refill on these empties," he said to RJ, then grinned at Devin. "You must be the fresh meat." He stuck out his hand. "Cage Weaver, prior Army Ranger, current full-time Broth-

erhood Protector and amazing busboy on the side."
He tilted his head toward the redhead. "My first
assignment was protecting Emily from a stalker,
which was a success, or Emily wouldn't be here
today. I've had other assignments since, proving
there is life after severing the military umbilical
cord."

Devin gripped the man's hand. "Thank you for
your service."

"Same to you. I hear you were 10th Special Forces
out of Fort Carson," Cage said. "We'll have to
compare deployments. We might've crossed paths at
some time or another."

"Make that another time," RJ said as she emptied
the tray and filled it with fresh drinks. "Your table is
looking thirsty."

Cage saluted RJ, lifted the tray as if it weighed
nothing and lifted his chin toward Devin. "You'll love
the job and the team. I couldn't have landed better in
this civilian world that doesn't really understand
what we did over there."

As Cage left with his tray of drinks, Jake returned
with his tray, having delivered the food and collected
the empties. He carried the tray back into the
kitchen. When he came back out, he leaned across
the bar and kissed RJ soundly. "Gunny's back. I'm
officially relieved of KP duty. Let me know if you
need any help out here."

She waved him away. "Go do your real job. I've

got this. And take Striker with you. He's decided to lie in the middle of the floor where I walk. Besides, he likes you more than me—the traitor that he is."

"He just wants your attention." Jake walked to the end of the bar, opened a gate and patted his leg. "Striker, come."

A golden Belgian Malinois trotted through the gate and sat at Jake's feet.

"When you're done talking with Devin," RJ said as she pulled a lever and filled a mug full of beer, "take Striker outside. It's been a while."

"I love a woman who can give commands like my BUD/S instructors. Sometimes, she scares me more than they did." He winked. "You know I love you."

"Yeah, yeah." RJ's lips twitched at the corners.

Jake turned to Devin. "Let's talk." He motioned toward an empty table in a corner not far from the bar.

Devin slid off the stool and walked again, doing his best not to limp.

Jake waited for Devin to take his seat before he eased himself into the one on the opposite side of the table. He stretched out the leg with the prosthetic and sighed. "Waiting tables and doing the short-order cook gig is hard work. I don't know how RJ and Gunny have done this for as long as they have."

"How often do you help out?" Devin asked.

"I live at the lodge, so I probably help more than

the others." He grinned toward RJ. "I also have a vested interest in the bartender. RJ is amazing. I can't keep up with the woman. She runs circles around me."

"Does that bother you?" Devin asked.

Jake frowned. "Bother me?" He laughed. "I learned early on that I don't have to keep up with RJ. She's like the Energizer bunny, and her batteries never run out. But she's always so focused on getting the job done she doesn't always recognize when she's in danger. She was my first assignment as a Brotherhood Protector. I had to keep her alive when someone tried to kill her."

He looked across the table at Devin. "In the process of protecting RJ, I learned a lot about her and Gunny. They're good people and work harder than anyone I've ever known. I also learned a lot about myself. I put my military training and skills to use in keeping her safe. I learned I could do a lot more than I thought I could."

Devin had to admit, if just to himself, he was impressed. Jake had lost his leg. Yet, he was still able to get around and had made himself useful by protecting RJ, a woman who looked like she could protect herself.

Jake glanced across the room at RJ. "The woman can most definitely take care of herself in most circumstances. But like SEALs are taught, no man is an island, and we aren't equipped with eyes in the backs of our heads. Teamwork saves lives. RJ needed someone who had her six. That was me."

"What exactly is it that Brotherhood Protectors do?" Devin asked.

His face now poker straight, Jake leaned toward Devin. "We do whatever it takes." His expression intense, Jake continued. "We might hire out as a bodyguard to provide personal protection for someone who has become the target of a stalker like Emily was." He nodded toward the redheaded waitress. "Her day job is as a psychologist at the VA hospital in Colorado Springs. One of her patients stalked her and would've killed her if Cage hadn't been assigned to protect her."

RJ arrived at the table with another glass of whiskey for Devin and what appeared to be a glass of water for Jake. She set the drinks on the table and returned to the bar without uttering a word.

Jake's lips twisted as he stared down at the water. "I gave up drinking when I came to work for Brotherhood Protectors. I was deep into the bottle when Hank Patterson sent Kujo to recruit me. If Kujo hadn't come to offer me a job, I doubt I'd be alive today."

"Hank Patterson, Kujo…" Devin shook his head. "Who are they?"

"Hank Patterson founded the Brotherhood Protectors up in Montana. He saw a need and knew our highly trained military folks had the skills to fill the need. Kujo, or Joseph Kuntz, is one of his team up in Montana. Besides protection services, we can perform extractions or rescues of people who've been involuntarily detained. We can be deployed anywhere in the world. Sometimes, we do what law enforcement can't or won't."

"And how is a man with a bad leg going to protect anyone? I can't run. I fall down a lot and take too long to get back up."

"But you get back up. You keep going. You don't give up. It's that kind of attitude, plus your combat training and experience, that makes you an asset to this organization."

"I don't know about being an asset," Devin muttered.

"All our members are prior military with years of experience conducting special operations," Jake said. "They don't just charge in and shoot everything that moves. They study the situation and make the best choice based on the information they have on hand. Again, tapping into their experience. Plus, we have access to a computer guru in the Montana headquarters and another computer expert in training in the Yellowstone office."

"How many branches of Brotherhood Protectors are there?" Devin asked.

"Three, for now." Jake grinned. "Knowing Hank, he's probably going to set up another region or district soon. The more people hear about us, the more work that comes in." He stopped talking and stared at Devin for a long moment. "I know it's a lot to take in and think about."

Devin nodded. "It is. But I haven't had a line of people knocking at my door, wanting me to come to work for them."

Jake nodded. "I know where you're coming from. Neither did I. I took this job as a last resort."

Devin frowned. "And now, you run this division?"

Jake laughed. "I know. It's hard to believe, even for me. But I've never been happier or more fulfilled."

"It all sounds too good to be true," Devin said.

Jake held up a hand. "Oh, it's not all babysitting wealthy people. You will use your combat training and survival skills. Make no doubt about that. Assignments can be highly dangerous. You have to be willing to take the risk and place your client's well-being above your own."

Devin nodded.

"So, do you want to think about it overnight?" Jake asked. "You can sleep on it. We can talk in the morning."

"Do you have an assignment waiting to be filled?" Devin asked.

Jake shook his head. "Not at this moment. All work has been allocated. But we can't wait for it to come in to hire good people. The work comes in waves. We're on the tail-end of a wave. It won't be long before more work comes our way. In the meantime, we'd have you familiarize yourself with what we have available to work with, like weapons communications equipment, tracking devices and computers."

"If I join the Brotherhood Protectors, I want to reserve the right to leave the group should I decide this isn't the kind of work I want to do." Devin met and held Jake's gaze.

Jake gave him a deep nod. "Fair enough. I only ask that you don't run out on your client. Coordinate a smooth transition to make the transfer easier on him or her."

Devin nodded. "Can do."

Jake's eyes widened, and a grin spread across his face. "Does this mean you're going to join us?"

Devin nodded.

"Sounds good," Jake said. "Sleep on it, to make sure this is what you want. If you change your mind, no worries. In the meantime, we'll move forward with bringing you on board."

"And you can sleep on it as well," Devin said. "Make sure I have what you need."

"Oh, we know what we're getting," Jake said with a grin. "You definitely have the skills we need."

Devin's mouth tightened. He wasn't entirely sure of what he might be getting into or if he could be of any real value. Then again, it was the only job he'd been offered besides the one-day security detail he'd performed for the rodeo.

He had no idea what he was getting into, nor did he really care. Committing to something was better than the limbo he'd been in since he'd been released from Walter Reed and shipped home.

Jake held out his hand. "Do we have a deal?"

Devin swallowed a rush of panic, gripped Jake's hand and said, "Deal."

CHAPTER 4

MAL FIDGETED, tugging at the short hem of the A-line dress Laurel had loaned her, insisting that it was perfect for a date night out to the movies. "How did I let you talk me into wearing a dress? It's so short my butt cheeks are cold."

Laurel slapped Mal's hands. "Stop. The dress comes down to mid-thigh, which is plenty long enough to cover your bottom. Besides, it's the latest style."

"On you, it might come to mid-thigh, but I'm a lot taller. So, on me, this dress isn't even close to mid-thigh." She tugged at the hem again and then straightened. "Wait a minute, if this short a dress is the style, why aren't you wearing a short one?"

Laurel ran her hand over the floaty floral lilac material draped over her body like it was made for her, falling to a swaying hem at mid-calf. "I wanted to be a little less risqué. I don't want Alan to think I'm easy."

Mal snorted. "So, you make me look like I'm easy? Some friend." She returned to tugging at the hem as they stood just inside the door to the flower shop. "I'd feel much better in jeans and my boots. It's not like I'm trying to attract anyone. Far from it."

"Speaking of attracting someone," Laurel crossed her arms over her chest, "where's this date you promised you'd scrounge up?"

Mal tipped her head toward the window. "That's him driving up right now."

Laurel's head snapped around.

The county sheriff's SUV pulled up to the curb. Sheriff Jim Faulkner stepped out of the vehicle, raised a hand in greeting then frowned. He pulled his cell phone out of his pocket and stared down at the screen. His frown deepened. He swiped the screen, pressed the phone to his ear and flashed his index finger toward Mal and Laurel, where they stood inside the glass door of Laurel's Florals.

Mal cast a glance toward her friend and laughed. "You should see your expression. It's priceless."

"This is a joke, right?" Laurel's brow furrowed.

"Nope." A smug smile tugged at Mal's lips.

Laurel glared at Mal. "Are you just trying to sabotage my date with Alan?"

"Not at all. But I did have a hard time finding someone to go to a movie with me on such short notice. I had to call in a favor, and Jim agreed to go with me." She grinned at the sheriff standing outside the shop, having a heated conversation with whoever had called. "He did change out of his uniform."

"You are trying to sabotage my date," Laurel said, a stubborn frown creasing her forehead. "I promise, Alan's a nice guy. You didn't have to subject him to the inquisition of County Sheriff Jim Faulkner."

Mal sighed, feeling bad about spoiling her friend's date. "I tried. Really, I did. It was a bit of a wake-up call to know I'm not all that."

Laurel's arms crossed over her chest. "I could have gotten Devin to come."

Mal shook her head vehemently. "Nope."

"Alan's a good guy," Laurel insisted.

"So's Jim." Mal tipped her head toward him. "He's got broad shoulders, narrow hips and a fine tight—"

"You forgot to tack on *for his age*," Laurel said, her lips twisting.

Mal lifted her chin and stared down her nose at the shorter woman. "Don't be so rude. Jim's forty-seven, not seventy-seven. He's in the prime of his life."

Laurel studied the sheriff. "I'm surprised he's still single."

"I know, right?" Mal laughed. "That man is damned good-looking. It's a miracle some marriage-minded woman hasn't snatched him off the market."

"I guess I never thought about it. I mean, he's

older...and the sheriff and all." She tilted her head. "Forty-seven and unmarried...hmmm."

Mal gave Laurel a sly smile. "Maybe he hasn't met the right girl. Since I'm free and single, maybe that girl is me." She jabbed her thumb at her chest.

Laurel's lips twisted. "Keep trying to fool yourself. He's fifteen years older than you. He could be your father."

"Only if he got my mother pregnant when he was fifteen."

Laurel pressed her hands over her ears. "I didn't hear that. I knew your mother. Ew."

Jim continued his conversation just outside the flower shop while Mal took the opportunity to admire the man, looking at him for the first time as something other than a friend.

He had it all going for him with his salt-and-pepper gray hair, green eyes and a dimple on his chin. Damn. He was a nice-looking man and a good friend.

Unfortunately, that was as far as her feelings went for Jim. She had a long way to go to get over her love for Devin. Maybe then she might be interested in Jim. But not now.

The sheriff ended his call, turned and smiled at them standing on the other side of the glass door.

Mal returned the smile and pushed open the door. "Hey, Jim."

"Mal," he said, his gaze raking over her from the

tip of her head to the strappy sandals on her feet. "You clean up well."

"Thank you." She gave him the same once-over. "You're not so bad yourself, out of uniform."

"Sometimes, I forget I have other clothes I can wear." He gave her a lopsided grin and then looked past her to Laurel. "I understand we're going to a movie."

"That was the plan," Laurel said. "Just me and my date." She cast a sharp, short glare in Mal's direction. "My friend here thinks I can't take care of myself."

Jim nodded toward Mal. "She's kind of right. Sometimes, you need someone to have your back. Especially with someone new in town that we know nothing about." His gaze met Mal's. "I do know he doesn't have a rap sheet. His record is clean. He didn't show up on any of my criminal databases."

Mal gave a slight shake of her head and pressed a finger to her lips. He wasn't supposed to tell Laurel.

Laurel spun toward Mal, glaring. "You did *not* have Jim run a background check on Alan."

Mal's cheeks heated. "I didn't ask him to run the check. He volunteered. Didn't you, Jim?"

Jim nodded. "It doesn't hurt to look. It beats going on a date with a serial killer."

Laurel flung her hands in the air. "Oh, I give up. I'm not a child."

Mal chuckled. "No, you are not, but you are well loved. We want to keep you around for a long time."

Mal wrapped her arms around Laurel. "You're my closest friend. I don't know what I'd do without you. You're my sister from another mister—especially since I don't have any parents to lean on."

Mal's parents had been gone since right after she'd graduated from high school. If not for Laurel, RJ and JoJo, she might have fallen apart. Devin had already left to join the Army.

Mal had missed him, but it wasn't until he'd come back the previous year that he'd finally seen her as more than just his kid sister's best friend and realized she was a full-grown woman. Everything had changed from that moment on. A spark had flared between them, igniting a fiery passion.

Pressing a hand to her suddenly thundering heart, Mal focused on their double date night. "Speaking of dates, where is this new guy who has taken my friend by storm? Please tell me he didn't stand you up on your second date."

Laurel shook her head. "No. He did mention something about getting a bigger car since it wasn't going to be just the two of us."

A large, black SUV pulled in beside the sheriff's vehicle, and Alan got out. His gaze ran over the sheriff's vehicle and then he looked up, a frown denting his brow. "Have any trouble at the flower shop today?" he asked. "Are you all right?"

Laurel shot a quick scowl at Mal, then turned a mega-watt fake smile at Alan. "No problems. It was a great day." She waved a hand toward Jim. "This is just Mal's date for tonight, Sheriff Jim Faulkner. Jim, meet Alan Croft. And Mal, this is Alan. Alan, Mallory Watts."

Alan shook hands with Mal and then started to reach for Jim's hand and stopped. "Should I be afraid?"

The sheriff shook his head with a grin. "No. I'm just Mal's date for the night because she couldn't get anyone else. So, I guess you could say I'm the consolation prize. Her last resort. The bottom of the barrel."

"Great," Mal said. "Now everyone in Fool's Gold will know I can't get a date."

"I wouldn't say you're a complete failure." The sheriff raised his hands, palms upward. "You got me."

Mal released a harrumph sound in response.

"If you're ready," Alan said, "we can head into Colorado Springs. I rented a vehicle big enough for all four of us. My little two-seater BMW wouldn't have done it. This way, we'll all be comfortable on the ride through the pass."

Jim leaned toward Mal and brushed a kiss across Mal's cheek. "You know I'm poking fun at you, right? You're a pretty girl who could have her pick of any man in this town if you set your mind to getting him."

That was where Jim was wrong. The one man she'd set her mind and heart on wanted nothing to do with her. "Thanks. And thanks for coming with us tonight." She hooked her arm through the crook of his elbow.

"Let's load up," Laurel said.

Jim held the door for Mal to climb into the SUV. She took longer than usual, doing her best to keep the hem of the dress covering her ass. "Can't believe I let her talk me into this damned dress," she murmured.

"For what it's worth, you look great," Jim grinned. "Like a regular girl."

While Mal adjusted her seatbelt in the backseat, Alan helped Laurel into the front passenger seat.

Once they were all in, Alan drove out onto Main Street, turning east. Soon, they were headed down the winding highway through Ute Pass on the way to Colorado Springs.

"So, Alan, you're new in town," Jim said, starting the conversation. "Where did you move from?"

"Idaho," Alan responded. "Up near Coeur D'Alene."

"Did you ever serve in the military?" Jim asked.

Alan looked back at Jim through the rearview mirror. "Eight years."

"Are you married?" Jim continued.

When Laurel reached back to smack Jim's leg, Mal clamped a hand over her mouth to keep from laughing out loud.

"Jim," Laurel bit out, her gaze shooting daggers, "this is not an inquisition."

"I know that." Jim stared back with a wide-eyed not-so-innocent look. "I'm just getting to know the new kid in town. He can ask me the same questions. No harm, no foul."

Alan's lips twitched. "Are you married, Jim?"

Jim shook his head. "No, sir. I haven't had the pleasure. And you haven't answered that same question."

Mal studied Alan's reflection in the rearview mirror. A shadow passed over his face before he answered. "Not married. Widowed."

"My condolences," Jim said. "It must be hard."

Alan's lips pressed tightly together. He paused for a moment before responding. "Yes, it is. Very hard."

"If you don't mind me asking," Mal started, "how long has it been?"

He stared at the road ahead. "A little over half a year."

"So, your interest in Laurel will likely be a rebound relationship," the sheriff stated.

Laurel gasped. "What is with you two? We're going on a date to see a movie. He's not asking to marry me, and I'm not saying yes. We're all just friends here, for Pete's sake." She crossed her arms over her chest and glared out the front windshield.

Jim sat back in his seat and met Mal's amused glance. "Too much?" he whispered.

"Definitely too much," Laurel said.

Mal laughed out loud. "I hope the movie is as entertaining as the conversation inside this vehicle."

The rest of the drive into the city was accomplished with lighter, less provocative topics. Mal steered the conversation toward the weather and the work she was doing with the horses on the Lucky Star Ranch. Jim fell in step, talking about the Denver Broncos.

Laurel relaxed and entertained them with some of the quirky encounters she'd had with customers.

Alan smiled and chimed in when appropriate.

Mal couldn't fault the guy. He held the door for Laurel and Mal, helped Laurel in and out of the SUV and paid for dinner for the four of them. Jim paid for the movie tickets to a romantic comedy about rival radio talk show hosts.

By the time they made it back to Fool's Gold, it was nearly midnight.

Mal was exhausted. She carefully slid out of the backseat, holding down the hem of her dress.

Once on the ground, she smothered a yawn and then grinned. "Well, that was fun. It also reminds me why I don't do it that often."

"That often?" Laurel laughed. "Try never."

Mal's eyebrows dipped. "I don't know when you get up in the morning, but my day begins at five-thirty. The animals can't wait. That means that midnight is three hours past my bedtime." She smothered another yawn and turned toward her truck. "I'd better go," she said. "My carriage awaits." She held out her hand to Jim.

He took it in his and gave it a gentle squeeze. "Get some rest."

She brought his hand up to cup her cheek. "Why can't I fall in love with someone as nice and considerate as you?" she asked.

"Because you gave your heart to Devin. He'll come around." Jim patted her cheek and dropped his hand to his side. "Give him time."

"You and Laurel are like an echo of each other. I get the message. Devin needs time, and I shouldn't give up on him." She sighed. "Thank you again for coming on this double date as my friend."

Jim nodded. "I'm here for you if you need a shoulder to cr—" he grinned, "—lean on."

"You're a good man, Jim Faulkner," Mal said, her voice cracking on the emotion welling up in her throat. "One day, you're going to meet the one for you. I hope that it's soon. You deserve to be happy."

He frowned slightly. "Who says I'm not happy?"

She tilted her head. "You're right. You don't have to have someone else in your life to complete you." Her chest tightened. "I know I can survive without Devin." She looked up at Jim with tears in her eyes. "I'd just prefer not to."

"Then don't give up on him. He's going through a rough patch. He'll come to his senses." Jim glanced at his watch. "You need to get home. I'll follow you out to your place."

Mal shook her head. "That's not necessary. I drive myself home every day. I don't need an escort."

Jim's lips tipped upward as he shook his head. "Humor me, will ya?"

Mal was too tired to argue. "Okay, but I'm an independent woman, capable of taking care of herself."

"Point noted," Jim said.

"Give me a minute. I need to get something out of Laurel's apartment." Mal turned to where Alan and Laurel sat on a bench in front of Laurel's Florals shop, their heads together, talking.

Laurel glanced up and smiled. "You need your clothes, don't you?"

Mal nodded. "I'd wait until tomorrow, but my boots are up there, and I need them."

"It's okay," Alan said. "We were just saying good-night." He stood and held out a hand to Laurel.

She laid her hand in his and let him pull her to her feet and into his arms.

Alan bent his head, brushed his lips across hers then stepped back. "Thank you for a wonderful evening."

"I enjoyed it," Laurel said, her cheeks flushed, her eyes reflecting the light from the street lamps. "Goodnight, Alan." She smiled shyly up at him. Then she turned and smiled at the sheriff. "Goodnight, Jim."

Jim dipped his head. "Goodnight, Laurel."

Laurel hooked her arm through Mal's and walked with her around the side of the flower shop to the stairs leading to the apartment above. As soon as she unlocked the door, Laurel pulled Mal through and closed it quickly. "So," she said, her eyes alight, "what did you think of Alan?"

Mal laughed. "He seems nice enough. He doesn't have a criminal record." She frowned. "What did he say he did for a living?"

"Something to do with security systems," Laurel said. "I like him."

Mal touched her friend's arm. "Just remember, his wife died not long ago. He might not be over her."

Laurel nodded. "I know. I'll keep that in mind. If he sticks around, I'll at least have someone to go to dinner with occasionally. If it leads to drinks in my apartment afterward...?" Laurel grinned. "Who knows where we can go from there."

Frowning, Mal moved around the room, gathering her clothes and boots. "Just don't be in a hurry to get intimate. Get to know him first."

"Yes, Mom," Laurel said, her tone dripping with sarcasm. "I'll be a good girl...until I'm not." She beamed.

Unable to be bossy or cranky with Laurel when

she seemed beside herself with happiness, Mal smiled. "It's nice to see you so happy."

Laurel chuckled. "I'm always happy. Life's too short to be anything else."

Mal shook her head. "How do you do that?"

Her friend stared at her. "Do what?"

"You're a constant ray of sunshine, no matter the circumstances." Her hands loaded with her things, Mal leaned into her friend and bussed her cheek with a kiss. "Don't ever change. It's what I love about you. No matter how bad things get, you always find the light."

Laurel stared into Mal's eyes. All the happiness seemed to have drained from her face. "It's because I've seen the dark, lived through it and never want to go back to that place again."

Mal dropped her boots on the floor and pulled Laurel into her arms. "One of these days, you'll have to tell me about your time in the Army. Whatever happened to you must've been pretty bad."

Laurel shivered in the circle of Mal's arm. "It wasn't all flowers and sunshine. That's for sure." She laughed, the sound hollow and forced. "You need to go home and get some sleep before you have to get up to feed the horses in the morning."

Mal picked up her boots, clutched her clothes to her chest and headed for the door. "If you need me for anything, I'm only a phone call away, and I can be here in less than fifteen minutes." She stopped at the door. "I can stay the night if you want me to."

"Thank you, Mal." Laurel smiled brightly. "I'm fine. But you're a good friend to ask."

Mal felt like Laurel was not her usual happy self, and she hated leaving her. She set her boots on the floor. "I'm staying."

"No." Laurel advanced on her, grabbed the boots from the floor and shoved them into Mal's arms. "I've come a long way from the mess I was when I came home all those years ago. I'm fine. Devin will be fine. But trust me, it takes time for all the wounds to heal, both physical and mental."

Mal stood for a moment longer. "I love you, Laurel Layne. You're the sister of my heart. I'd do anything for you."

"I know," she said with her smile that lit the room. "Love of my family and friends and a purpose are what got me through it all and brought me to where I am today." She hugged Mal and turned her around. "Go home and rest."

Mal stepped out onto the upper landing. When she turned back, Laurel had the door half-closed. "Goodnight, Mal."

"Goodnight, Laurel," Mal replied as Laurel closed the door. The metal clicking of the lock engaging reassured Mal only slightly.

As she descended the stairs, Mal wondered if Laurel's perpetual optimism was an act to cover the horrors she'd experienced on her last deployment with the Army.

She'd only skimmed over what had happened, refusing to go into the details. All Mal knew was that Laurel had been captured by the Taliban and managed to escape. What occurred between her capture and escape, only Laurel, her commanding officer and her psychiatrist knew. Laurel hadn't offered to share the details with Mal. As far as she knew, Laurel hadn't even shared the ordeal with her brother.

Mal hadn't pushed her for more information. Her friend didn't need to rehash the horror to appease Mal's curiosity.

With her clothes and boots in hand, Mal descended the stairs and found Jim waiting at the bottom. "Sorry. That took a little longer than I expected. You really don't have to follow me out to my place."

He held up his hand without saying a word.

"Right," she said. "You'd do it anyway." Mal looked past him. "Alan left?"

"Yup. He said something about a project he had to work on tomorrow." Jim walked with her to her truck and opened the back door so that she could place her things on the backseat.

Mal dumped the clothes and boots on the seat, wishing she'd taken the time to change in Laurel's apartment. Climbing into the truck wasn't the most graceful thing to do in a short dress that barely covered her important parts.

Jim stood there, waiting for her to get in the truck. Mal sighed and did her best to climb in without mooning the man.

Once she'd settled in the seat and adjusted her hem, she smiled at Jim. "Thanks. I can take it from here."

He chuckled. "More used to jeans and boots, aren't you?"

She rolled her eyes. "The dress was Laurel's idea."

"You looked great in it. Thanks for inviting me along."

"Thanks for coming. You're a good friend, Jim."

"That's me. Your friend, Jim. I'm there when you need me." He reached for her hand and held it in his, staring down at her knuckles. "And if you ever fall out of love with Devin Layne, I'll still be there when you need me." He lifted his gaze to meet hers.

Mal sucked in her breath at the intensity of Jim's stare. He'd been her friend for years, and she'd never considered him anything else.

However, by the look in his eyes, his thoughts of her were more than friendly.

Mal pulled her hand free. "I...I...didn't know."

Jim's lips stretched into a tight smile. "And now you're uncomfortable. My apologies. I just wanted you to know you have other options if things fall through with Devin. No pressure. Just another option." He closed her door, strode to his service vehicle, climbed in and waited for her to leave her parking space and head home.

Stunned and confused, Mal's gaze followed him until he got into his vehicle. Then she shook her head, started her engine and pulled out onto Main Street.

Jim Faulkner?

Again, she shook her head. He was her friend. Never had she considered him as anything more. Probably, as Laurel had pointed out, because of their age difference. Still, the older they got, the less the gap meant. Sure, if she'd been fifteen and he'd been thirty, that would be just wrong.

Sheriff Jim Faulkner?

"No," she murmured. When he'd held her hand in his, she'd felt nothing more than comfort. No spark. No surge of longing so intense she couldn't catch her breath.

Not like when she was with Devin.

But didn't sparks fade?

She glanced in her rearview mirror at the official law enforcement vehicle behind her and wondered what it would be like to love a sheriff.

An image of Devin on horseback as he'd appeared yesterday flashed through her mind. Heat flooded her body, coiling hotter at her core.

Devin Layne was so much a part of her soul that Mal couldn't imagine any other man sharing her life. Her chest tightened as she recalled Devin's rejection.

Laurel and Jim had been in the military, deployed to war-torn countries and lived through the stress of battle. They'd both said the same thing. Give Devin time to recover from his physical and mental wounds. Don't give up on him.

Another glance in the mirror made Mal more resolute. Though she didn't feel anything other than friendship for Jim, it felt good to know she was admired and possibly loved by another male. Her rough, cowgirl exterior didn't scare Jim.

At one time, her independence and strength hadn't scared Devin. Now, it appeared to intimidate him and make him feel less of a man.

Mal couldn't change who she was. But she could wait for him to heal on the inside and outside.

She just hoped it was soon. Mal wasn't a very patient person.

As Mal pulled into her driveway, Jim slowed to a stop at the curb and waited for her to get out and walk into her little cottage. She'd rented the place after her parents had died, not wanting to burden her friends and their families by staying with them.

After high school graduation, Mal had transitioned from part-time to full-time employment with the Lucky Star Ranch, training horses and caring for livestock.

She fished her key out of her pocket, inserted it

into the lock and pushed open the door. After she reached in to flip the light switch, she turned. Without making eye contact, she waved toward Jim and dove into her home.

Once inside, she slammed the door shut and leaned her back against it.

Jim Faulkner had a thing for her.

He was nice, handsome and an all-around good guy. Why not Jim?

Mal sighed and pushed away from the door. It could never be Jim because, no matter how much she wanted to forget Devin and move on, the former Green Beret held her heart, mind and soul.

"So, what are you going to do about it?" she asked herself aloud.

Mal marched through her cottage to her bedroom and into the adjoining bathroom. "I'm going to win him back." She yanked back the shower curtain, turned on the water with a determined flick of her wrist and stood with her fists on her hips while the cool spray warmed. How she'd win him back, she didn't have a clue. But she was smart. When she set her mind to something, she made it happen.

It was nice to know someone out there loved her even if Devin didn't. Still, second best wasn't good enough when it came to matters of the heart.

CHAPTER 5

Devin was sound asleep when his cell phone chirped the next day. He rolled over and blinked at the screen. Laurel's name filled the small space. Sunlight streamed through the open curtain, filling the room with light. What the hell time was it? A glance at the clock made him frown as he grabbed for the incessantly chirping phone.

"What?" he croaked.

"Devin, I hate to bother you, but…" his sister's voice wavered, "especially since I'm not sure there's a problem. It's just…something isn't right."

Devin sat up in the bed, his frown deepening. The fog of sleep took a moment to clear. "What do you mean something isn't right?"

"I was super busy this morning in the shop, getting orders out. When I caught a break, I dashed upstairs to my apartment and…well…something's different."

"You're not making sense."

His sister laughed shakily. "I know. And it might not be anything, but when you get a chance, will you come by?"

He sighed. "Give me twenty minutes."

"I'll be in the shop working. Thanks," she said.

He started to end the call when Laurel continued.

"And, Devin," she said, "it's nice to have my big brother home again."

She ended the call.

Fully awake now, Devin swung out of bed, the usual pain shooting up his leg as his foot hit the floor. Powering through the jolt, he hurried into the adjoining bathroom. After a quick shower, he ran a comb through his hair and brushed his teeth.

His sister's call had him slightly worried. She'd been on her own for some time and was stubbornly independent. After what she'd experienced at the hands of the Taliban, she'd come a long way. If something didn't feel right to her…hell…something wasn't right.

Devin pulled on his jeans and boots, dragged a T-shirt over his head and limped out of his house to his truck.

The drive into town usually took fifteen minutes. Instead, he accomplished the same journey in ten, pushing past the posted speed limit while a knot formed in his empty gut.

When he arrived in front of Laurel's Florals, he shoved the shift into park and slid out of the truck onto the ground. He'd become used to the constant pain in his leg. It was more annoying than completely debilitating as it had been at the beginning of his rehabilitation.

Laurel met him at the door and stepped out into the warm Colorado sunshine. "Thanks for coming, though I feel kind of silly about it. I'm sure it's nothing."

"I'm here now. Show me what's got you feeling weird."

She grimaced. "Okay." Laurel led the way around the side of the building to the stairs leading up to her apartment. The air was cooler in the shadowed alley between the florist shop and the art gallery next to it.

Laurel unlocked the door, stepped inside her neat little apartment and waited just inside the door for Devin to enter. "Like I said, I came up for a break, and it just felt off in here. I can't quite put my finger on it."

Devin sniffed the air. As far as he could tell, there wasn't a gas leak. "You need to be a little more specific. How is it off in here?"

She pointed to the table in the entryway, her brow puckered. "It's little things like that photo of you, me and our parents."

Devin stared at the framed photograph taken when he and Laurel were kids, and their parents were still alive and very much a part of their lives. His chest tightened. He missed them. "What about the picture?"

"I keep that photo on a shelf near the television. I don't recall moving it to this table near the door."

"Could you have done it when you were cleaning and forgot to put it back?"

She shook her head. "I wouldn't have carried it clear across the room. When I dust, I usually move it to another shelf and put it right back when I'm done."

"Is that the only thing that's worrying you? Was anything taken?"

Laurel shook her head. "As far as I can tell, nothing was taken, which would make more sense." She crossed to the far side of the couch. A picture frame lay face-down on the end table. "I'm pretty certain that photograph wasn't lying like that when I left this morning." She walked into her bedroom and pointed to the neatly made bed. "And I swear I didn't make my bed this morning. I woke up late because we were out so late last night. I was in a hurry to get down to the shop."

"Do you have a cleaning service?" Devin shook his head as he said the words.

Laurel snorted. "This place isn't big enough to need a service. I usually leave it neat and clean. Just not this morning because of our late night."

"Has anyone else been in your apartment recently?"

"Not since late last night." Laurel's eyebrows drew together. "Mal came in to collect her clothes and boots."

Devin's heart skipped a beat. "Mal?"

"I made her wear one of my dresses on our double date. She left her clothes here and collected them when we got back."

"Could she have moved the photographs?"

Laurel's lips twisted. "I don't think so. She was only here to get her clothes." She turned back to the bed. "And she wasn't here this morning to make my bed."

"Does she have a key to your apartment?"

"No," Laurel said. "The only other person with a key to my apartment is you."

His sister had given him the key when he'd come back into town. Devin had that key on his keychain in his pocket.

"Are you sure you locked your door this morning?" he asked.

"I was in a hurry, but I'm very careful about locking my doors. We might be a small town, but, being a single female, I don't take any chances."

Devin walked back into the living room, pulled a tissue from a box on the end table and used it to flip the facedown photo over. His heart pinched hard in his chest. It was a picture of him and Mal the day he'd proposed to her. Her fresh, clean face smiled up at a happier Devin.

Laurel had insisted that he do it right and with someone there to photograph the event.

He'd taken her to the top of Pike's Peak and proposed there.

His sister had gone up before them. She'd stayed out of sight when he and Mal had arrived. She'd snapped several photos of his proposal and Mal's acceptance. The photograph he stared down at was his favorite. Mal had been so happy. Hell, so had he.

As he set the framed photograph back on the table, face down, his jaw hardened, and he turned away. "Is it possible that Mal knocked the photo over when she was here last night?" After he'd called off their engagement, Devin wouldn't be surprised if Mal had burned that photograph of the two of them. "And maybe she moved the other photo while she was here? You said you were out on a double date last night. Maybe she didn't want her date to see this one."

Laurel had followed Devin, pausing in the bedroom doorway. "Our dates didn't come up to my apartment after we went out for dinner and a movie in the Springs. It was just me and Mal who'd come up here when we got back. We left Alan and Mal's date in front of the shop." Laurel's lips twisted into a wry grin. "As it was, I was supposed to go on the date, just

Alan and me. Mal insisted on going along to check out Alan. I said no way. When she suggested we go on a double date, I agreed."

Devin's blood burned at the thought of Mal going out with someone else. Memories of the dates he'd taken her on flooded his mind, making his gut knot. They'd known each other for years, but it wasn't until he'd come back on leave that he'd seen her as more than just his sister's friend. Mal had grown into a beautiful young woman. He couldn't imagine anyone else with Mal besides him. It hurt to know she'd gone out with someone else so soon after their breakup.

Though he wanted to know whom Mal took as her date, he refused to ask.

Silence stretched between him and his sister.

Laurel crossed her arms over her chest. "You're not going to ask me who Mal's date was, are you?"

He turned away from the upside-down photograph and crossed the living room, putting as much space between him and their happier times together. "It's none of my business."

"Sheriff Faulkner," Laurel said.

"Huh?" Devin shot a glance toward his sister.

"Her date was Jim Faulkner." Laurel raised her eyebrows. "You know…Sheriff Jim Faulkner."

"Isn't he old enough to be her father?"

"He's only fifteen years older than Mal, and he's a

very good-looking man and a fine, upstanding citizen. And just in case you wondered, the good sheriff did interrogate my date to make sure he was worthy of me. Not that you asked or cared."

Reining in his thoughts of the double date the night before, Devin glanced around the apartment. "Whatever. Back to your potential break-in... Was there any sign of forced entry?"

Laurel shook her head. "None. I lock the door every time I leave my apartment. When I came up on break a little while ago, I unlocked the door. So, it *was* locked."

"Maybe you should call the sheriff's department and have them dust for prints."

Laurel bit her bottom lip. "I hesitate to do that." She turned and walked to the window overlooking Main Street. "What if I did all those things and just don't remember?"

Devin followed her to the window, gripped her arms and turned her to face him. "Have you had any memory lapses since your return from Afghanistan? PTSD can do strange things to your mind."

"Don't we know," Laurel's voice broke on what might have been a sob. Her eyes filled with moisture. "You know I'm always here for you."

His lips pressed together. "We're not talking about me."

"I know what you're going through." She reached up and cupped her brother's cheek. "It wasn't easy fitting back into Fool's Gold. I wasn't sure I would. But, over time, I did. What happened to us is in the past. We have our futures to look forward to."

Devin's future without Mal seemed bleak.

"You didn't have to push her away," Laurel said softly.

His jaw hardened. "She deserves better. I don't want her to have to take care of me for the rest of my life. She needs someone strong and healthy like she is."

Laurel cocked an eyebrow, her lip curling at the corner. "Like Sheriff Faulkner?"

Devin dropped his hands from Laurel's arms, his teeth clenching.

"He's a good man," Laurel murmured, digging the knife deeper into Devin's chest. "He could make her happy."

"All that matters is that Mal is happy." He walked away from his sister. "I'll stop by the sheriff's department and get them to come here and dust for fingerprints. I'll make sure they keep it on the down-low. Better safe than sorry." He opened the door and stepped out onto the landing.

"Thank you, Devin," Laurel called out.

When he started to shut the door, her voice stopped him.

"And Devin...don't give up on Mal. You're worth loving. Don't take that away from her."

"Not your business," he said as he closed the door

between them.

As he eased himself down the staircase, he regretted promising to go to the sheriff's department. With his luck, he'd run into Mal's date from the night before. That was about the last thing he wanted to do, right up there with having bamboo shoots rammed beneath his fingernails.

But he'd promised. If it made Laurel feel better, he'd wade through a pond full of hungry alligators. His sister had been through enough in her short life. Moving photographs and a self-making bed were unsettling when you didn't remember doing them.

He wondered if Laurel was having memory lapses. Maybe he'd get hold of Cage's woman—the one who worked as a psychologist at the VA hospital and ask if PTSD could cause memory gaps.

The other explanation was more unsettling. What if someone had actually broken into Laurel's apartment and moved things around? Why would someone do that? What would motivate someone to do that?

The sheriff's office wasn't far. He drove anyway, meaning to head out to Lost Valley Ranch afterward to check in with Jake and start learning the ropes of the job of being a Brotherhood Protector. His gut knotted at the thought of having to protect someone. If that someone was swift on their feet, Devin would have a helluva a time keeping up.

Once he'd parked outside the sheriff's office, he

sucked in a deep breath, shoved open his truck door and eased out of the driver's seat onto the ground. He hadn't even shut his door when a sheriff's vehicle pulled into the parking lot and stopped in the space beside him.

Sheriff Faulkner climbed out of the SUV and rounded the hood of his vehicle. "Devin Layne," he said, holding out his hand, "Heard you were back in town. My dispatch told me you provided security detail for the rodeo while it was in town."

Devin gritted his teeth and shook the man's hand when he really wanted to punch the guy in his handsome, silver-fox kind of face. Laurel was right. He was good-looking. Worse, he was able-bodied and appeared to be in excellent shape, physically and mentally.

"I did ride security for the rodeo," Devin managed to say.

"Glad you did. It saved the department from having to provide support. We're shorthanded as it is." The sheriff dropped his hand and grinned. "I don't suppose you'd like to come to work for the sheriff's department, would you?"

Devin shook his head. "No, thank you. Got a job." He was glad he could say that, even though he wasn't quite sure he would be able to keep it. Not with a bum leg.

Faulkner looked toward the sheriff's office. "Are you here on business? Anything I can help you with?"

He bit his tongue to keep from saying, *You can keep the hell away from Mal.* "As a matter of fact, there is something you can help me with." He glanced around at people walking along the sidewalks, unwilling to broach the subject in the open.

"Would you like to step into my office?" the sheriff asked.

Damn. The man had it all going for him. Handsome, able-bodied and polite. He nodded. "I'd prefer to speak to you alone."

"We can do that." Sheriff Faulkner opened the door and held it for Devin.

Doing his best not to limp, Devin strode through the door, his head held high.

The sheriff greeted the deputy behind the desk and kept walking, leading the way to an office in the back. Once they'd both cleared the door, he closed it behind him. "Have a seat."

Devin sat in a chair facing the desk.

The sheriff took a seat behind the desk and leaned forward. "What can I help you with?"

"My sister," Devin said.

"Your sister?" Faulkner sat back in his chair and grinned. "I have to admit, I was a little nervous when you wanted to speak to me alone. I thought you were going to say something about my date with Mal last night."

Oh, he wanted to say a lot about Faulkner's date with Mal. Instead, he counted to three and focused on why he'd come. "Laurel thinks someone was in her apartment today while she was working below in the shop. It's got her spooked."

The sheriff frowned. "Were there any signs of forced entry? Is anything missing?"

Devin shook his head and told Faulkner what he'd observed and what his sister had told him. "My sister didn't want to go to the sheriff's office because she didn't want to make a big deal out of it, just in case she had some strange lapse in her memory."

The sheriff's frown deepened. "Does she have lapses in her memory often?"

"Not that we know of. But she is prior military and was captured and tortured by the Taliban. She suffers from PTSD."

Faulkner nodded. "And you never know how PTSD might manifest in each individual. Some of my buddies from my time in service struggle every day with PTSD. One ended up committing suicide."

Faulkner had been in the military. Devin should have recognized it by the way he carried himself and the respect he showed others. "What branch?"

"Marine Corps," the sheriff said, sitting up a little taller in his chair.

"Spec Ops?" Devin guessed.

The older man nodded. "Marine Force Recon. I retired after twenty-five years. Had to make room for the younger men."

One more reason to admire the man. Damn. He was perfect for Mal.

Devin's chest ached. He couldn't hate the man, and he needed his help.

"I'll come by myself and dust for fingerprints. Does she have a surveillance system? Any cameras around her place?"

Devin shook his head. "No, but I'll check into getting one installed."

"It's a good idea." Sheriff Faulkner pushed to his feet. "Is that all you needed?"

Devin stood, ignoring the pain of putting weight on his leg. "Laurel wants to keep things quiet, especially if she is having memory lapses."

"I understand. Just in case, I'll keep an eye on her place whenever I drive by."

"Thank you." Devin held out his hand. "And thank you for your service."

The man gripped his hand and stared into his eyes. "Thank you for your service. I'll get the kit and head over to Laurel's place. I'll need your prints, Laurel's and Mal's to rule everyone out."

"I'll follow you back to the shop. You can print me there." Devin opened the door, stepped out into the hallway and turned toward the exit.

"I'll see you there," the sheriff said and turned in the opposite direction.

Devin left the sheriff's office feeling better and worse all at once. Better that the sheriff would fingerprint Laurel's apartment. Worse because the sheriff was a likable guy. Someone who could make Mal happy.

He drove back to Laurel's shop and found her in the back, finishing a flower arrangement.

She set the vase aside, brushed her hands over her apron and led the way up to her apartment.

True to his word, the sheriff arrived minutes later and took their fingerprints before dusting the picture frames and doorknobs. Next, he dusted the windowsill in case an intruder had entered from that direction. When he was done, he left, promising to let them know what, if anything, he found.

Devin stayed behind with Laurel. "He may or may not find anything."

Laurel sighed. "It's better than doing nothing."

"I'm going out to Lost Valley Ranch to talk with Jake Cogburn."

Laurel's face brightened. "You took the job with the Brotherhood Protectors?"

Devin nodded. "I don't know that I'll be of any use to them, but it beats being unemployed."

Laurel shook her head. "You'll be great. They've done so much for people around here. Just ask RJ, JoJo and Emily."

"Has it been that crazy around here while I was gone?" he asked.

She nodded. "You'd be surprised. For a small town, we've had our share of crime."

"Which reminds me. We need to install a video surveillance system."

Laurel grimaced. "I've been meaning to do that, just haven't had the time. Business has been booming, and I can barely keep up with it."

"I'll see what I can do," Devin promised.

They left her apartment together. Devin watched as Laurel locked the door and pocketed her keys in her apron.

"You know, you can stay out at the ranch with me if you don't feel comfortable being in your apartment at night," he offered.

She smiled. "I might do that. I'll see how I feel tonight."

At the bottom of the stairs, he hugged his sister. "Be extra aware of your surroundings and the people in them. You're the only sister I've got."

She wrapped her arms around his waist and squeezed hard. "Same goes for you. I almost lost you. I'm glad you're back home." She stepped back. "Oh, I meant to tell you that you might have noticed some cattle on the ranch."

"I thought I saw some out in one of the far fields. Is one of the fences down? I haven't gotten around to checking. I had to borrow a horse for security duty at the rodeo, and I'm not sure any of the ATVs still run. They've been sitting up for a long time."

Laurel shook her head. "No need to worry right away. The fences should be intact. The cattle belong to Mal. I let her run them on the place to keep the agriculture exemption while you've been away. She checks on them at least once a week. You might see her out in the fields. Of course, it's up to you whether you want her to continue to run her cattle on your place. I mean, since you two aren't engaged anymore, it might be...awkward. And you might want to build your own herd now that you're back."

He hadn't thought that far ahead. "No reason to change things. The cattle can stay. I need time to get my bearings before I start anything on the ranch."

Laurel smiled. "You have all the time in the world. You're home. That's what matters."

A woman walked past them and entered the shop.

"That's my cue," Laure said. "I'd better get back to work."

"Call me any time," Devin said. "I'm here for you."

"I'm sorry you can't continue your career with the Army, but the selfish side of me is glad you're home." She leaned up, kissed his cheek and ducked into her shop.

Devin climbed into his truck, his gaze on the sign over the shop. Laurel's Florals. He smiled, happy for his little sister's success. She'd done it all without his help. However, now that he was back, she wasn't alone. He'd help however he could. To start, he'd make sure she had a surveillance system installed. And maybe it was time to replace her locks.

If someone had gotten into her apartment, what

had been the purpose? Nothing was missing. All they had accomplished was to scare her. If that was the goal...they'd succeeded.

CHAPTER 6

Devin drove to the Lost Valley Ranch to meet with his new boss, Jake Cogburn.

His visit with Sheriff Faulkner had been the kick in the pants he'd needed to stop feeling sorry for himself and get on with living. Not that the sheriff had given him a pep talk or anything. But he was an example of a success story.

Many men and women who left the military found it difficult to transition into civilian life. Sheriff Faulkner and Laurel had done it right.

Devin didn't know Faulkner's military record, but if he'd been a member of Marine Force Recon, he'd been in the thick of battles, watched people die and might have sustained injuries.

The same went for Jake Cogburn. The man had lost a leg. He'd admitted to turning to alcohol to deal with his depression. Now, he was in charge of the

Colorado division of the Brotherhood Protectors, with men reporting to him and cases to assign. He'd turned himself around and gotten to work.

For the first time since he'd been injured and medically retired from the army, Devin felt a glimmer of hope. That huge stab of jealousy might have been even more of a kick in the pants than anything else.

If those two men could turn their lives around and be productive, maybe Devin would have a chance to do the same.

As he pulled up in front of the lodge, movement at the front entrance caught his attention.

Gunny stepped out onto the front porch, stretched and headed down the steps. When he spotted Devin getting out of his truck, he waved. "If you're looking for Jake, he's in the basement." The old Marine hurried past him to the path through the woods that led to the Watering Hole.

"Do you need help tonight?" Devin asked.

Gunny called out over his shoulder, "No, thank you. Should be a slow night. Might even close early."

Devin entered the lodge, passed through the great room, the dining room and pushed the swinging door into the kitchen.

RJ stood in front of the oven with the door open. The scent of cookies filled the air. "Just in time for some of my famous chocolate chip cookies." She grinned. "Jake's in the war room. I'll bring the cookies down once they've cooled."

Devin inhaled deeply as he passed through the kitchen. "They smell really good."

"They taste even better." RJ laid the tray of cookies on a trivet and put another tray of unbaked cookies into the oven.

Devin opened the door to the basement and descended into the operations center of the Colorado division of the Brotherhood Protectors. It felt like stepping into a new chapter of his life. He hoped he lived up to the reputation they'd apparently built in the short time they'd been in operation in the area.

Jake glanced up from where he stood with Cage and a man with sandy blond hair and gray eyes who was vaguely familiar to Devin.

They'd been gathered around the far end of the conference table in the center of the room.

"Daredevil Layne," Jake called out as he straightened. "You've met Cage. And you know Max Thornton.

Devin approached the trio. He nodded toward Cage and held out his hand to Thornton. "I thought you looked familiar. Didn't recognize you out of uniform."

Max chuckled. "I know what you mean. We look like completely different people out of the military environment." He took Devin's hand and pulled him into a bear hug. "Good to see you. It's been a day or two." When he released Devin, Thorn ran his gaze the length of Devin from head to toe. "You made it through the torture of rehab, and you're standing on two feet. I consider that a win."

"Still have work to do on mobility, but I'm off the pain meds," Devin confessed.

"Damned pain meds will suck you down the rabbit hole if you let them. If not pain, then alcohol. It's good that you dodged that bullet." Jake clapped Devin's back. "Glad you're joining us."

"Thanks for being persistent. I hope I live up to your expectations." Devin glanced around the room. "I meant to be here earlier, but I had a call from my sister I couldn't ignore."

Jake's brow dipped. "Everything all right with our favorite florist?"

Devin shrugged. "I think so, but I wanted to make sure." Then because he knew these men would understand Laurel's concerns, he shared what had happened, explaining what he'd done in response.

Jake's eyes narrowed. "How many times have you had a gut feeling?"

"All too often, especially going into a bad situation," Devin said.

Jake crossed his arms over his chest. "And how often was your gut right?"

"Every time." Devin noted how Cage and Thorn both nodded. "To the point that I listened to my gut and acted accordingly."

"My instinct saved my ass more times than I can count," Jake said. "You did right to call in the sheriff."

"Part of me hopes he doesn't find anything, and this is all just a weird incident Laurel and I will laugh about over beer.

"Until then, I'll work on making her place more secure." He drew in a deep breath and let it out. "Tell me about what you have here. RJ called this the war room."

"War room, operations center, nucleus..." Jake shrugged. "It's like a tactical operations center where we can meet to discuss a case or an operation needing multiple agents' involvement."

He pointed to the array of computer monitors in one corner and a bank of laptops. "We have the latest computers and can connect with Hank Patterson and his people in Eagle Rock and West Yellowstone, Montana."

"Impressive," Devin commented.

Jake continued. "We have access to his computer guy, Swede, who can find the most obscure data or hack his way into just about any database in the world. If he's not around, his backup is out of West Yellowstone, a woman named Kyla, who could probably rival any of our former special ops guys with her marksmanship and combat skills."

"Hank only brings the best into the Brotherhood," Thorn added.

"Then why me?" Devin asked. "I'm not up to my physical best."

Jake tapped the side of his head. "You have years of training and knowledge about tactics, maneuvers and combat skills. You can't teach that stuff in a classroom."

"You have to live it," Cage said. "All the people hired into the Brotherhood Protectors have combat experience."

"That's right," Thorn said. "We've breached enemy compounds to take out terrorists, extracted important people from enemy control or rescued captives."

Jake crossed his arms over his chest. "We've worked in some of the most hostile environments and infiltrated compounds to gather intelligence, leaving our enemy unaware of our presence."

"We did all that while we were strong and agile," Devin argued.

"And we learned to compensate for any weaknesses along the way," Jake said. "What you need is your first assignment. One that will help you understand your value and worth as a Brotherhood Protector in the civilian world. Unfortunately, all cases have been assigned to our current staff. We have a few clients who are considering our services. Until they commit, we don't have anything for you to sink your teeth into."

Devin was torn between being disappointed and relieved. "In the meantime, I'd like to get a surveillance system installed at my sister's shop and apartment. If she isn't hallucinating or having memory lapses, someone's messing with her."

Jake's eyes narrowed. "By all means. I can recommend a couple of systems we've used with some of our clients."

Devin's cell phone vibrated in his pocket. "Excuse me." He pulled the phone out of his pocket and frowned down at a number he didn't recognize. He almost didn't answer, thinking it might be a spam call, but changed his mind. The way things were going, it might be important.

"Layne here," he answered.

"Devin Layne?" a female voice said into his ear.

"That's me," he responded, ready to end the call if she tried to sell him a car warranty.

"This is Brandy Simpson, your sister's assistant. I'm at the Mountain Medical center with Laurel."

Devin's pulse kicked up. "What's wrong?"

"She wanted me to call and tell you she's all right, but she might need you to come pick her up when they're done stitching her hand."

"Stitching her hand?"

"Here," Brandy said. "She wants to talk to you. I'll hold the phone for her."

"Devin," Laurel's voice filled his ear.

"Laurel, what's this about stitches on your hand?"

"I didn't look everywhere in my apartment."

"What do you mean?"

"I was supposed to go to girls' night out at the casino with Brandy, Emily and JoJo. I ran up to get a quick shower. I had just finished washing my hair and reached for my loofah. Something sliced into my palm and fingers." She paused. "Devin, I found a razor blade embedded in my freakin' loofah. Whoever was in my apartment today planted that razorblade. If you don't mind, I want to stay at the ranch with you tonight."

"Damn right, you will. I'm coming to the hospital to get you."

"Thanks, Devin," his sister said. "I'm glad you're back."

"Devin, it's Brandy again," Laurel's assistant said. "I'll stay with Laurel until you get here. She'll need you to run by her apartment for some clothes. I helped her into a robe, but that's all she has on right now."

"If you can hold on with her for a few more minutes, I want to call the sheriff and have him swing by the apartment."

"I can do that," Brandy said. "See you when I see you." She ended the call.

Devin turned to Jake. "I have to go. It appears that the intruder we weren't sure was an intruder really was. He planted a razor blade in her loofah sponge. She's at the Mountain Medical Clinic getting stitches in her hand."

Jake swore. "I'm going with you."

Devin took the stairs up to the kitchen two at a time, ignoring the pain knifing through his calf and knee. He half-ran and limped past RJ as she filled a platter full of chocolate chip cookies.

"What's going on?" she asked.

Jake slowed long enough to answer, "Laurel is at the medical clinic. Someone spiked her loofah with a razor blade."

"Holy hell. Is she all right?"

"She's getting stitches in her hand."

"What can I do to help?" she asked.

"Call Sheriff Faulkner and tell him to meet me at Laurel's apartment," Devin called out.

"On it," RJ said, reaching for the phone on the wall.

Devin pushed through the swinging door, hurried past dining tables and the great room, and burst through the lodge doors onto the porch.

By the time he made it to his truck, Jake was coming out of the lodge. Devin lowered his window. "I'm stopping at Laurel's apartment first."

Jake nodded. "I'll go straight to the medical clinic and stay with Laurel until you get there."

Devin hit the accelerator and blew out of the parking lot and down the road leading out of the ranch. When he reached the highway, he floored the accelerator and raced toward Fool's Gold. The sun had dropped below the surrounding peaks, throwing everything into a hazy dusk.

As he neared Fool's Gold, he slowed and turned left onto Main Street.

The sheriff's SUV was parked outside Laurel's Florals. Sheriff Faulkner stood at the bottom of the steps leading up to Laurel's upstairs apartment.

Devin skidded to a stop, slammed the shift into park and flung open his door. When he dropped to the ground, his leg gave out, and he would have fallen had he not caught himself on the door.

"I don't have time for this shit," he muttered, pulled himself upright and hurried toward the sheriff.

"I came as soon as I got the call," Faulkner said. "Do you have a key?"

"I do." Devin led the way up the stairs and unlocked the door. When he flipped on the light, the first thing he saw was the trail of blood across the floor, leading all the way through the living room into the bedroom.

Devin did his best not to step in it as he passed through the bedroom to the bathroom. The shower curtain had a bloody handprint, and the tub was filled with even more blood. Near the drain was a baby-blue loofah covered in Laurel's blood.

Anger surged through Devin. "So much damn blood."

Sheriff Faulkner pulled latex gloves from his pocket and fit his hands into them. From his other pocket, he brought out a gallon-sized plastic bag. He reached into the tub and carefully lifted the loofah, turning it over to reveal the shiny corner of a razor blade. "We didn't even think to look in the shower for anything disturbed."

"The bastard banked on that," Devin said through gritted teeth.

"She's lucky she only cut her hand. If she'd brought it up to her face..." The sheriff shook his head.

Devin's fists clenched. Anger burned along with frustration. He wanted to hit someone. "What kind of sadistic bastard would do this?"

Faulkner's lips pressed together. "Has she made anyone mad lately?"

"Laurel?" Devin snorted. "She's the most opti-mistic, happy person I know."

"No kidding. You can always count on her to smile and say hello. Her business is booming because of her sunny disposition. I can't imagine anyone being mad at her."

"Can I leave you here to finish up?" Devin asked. "I want to get to the medical clinic."

"Go. I'll lock up when I leave. She's not coming back here tonight, is she?"

Devin shook his head. "No. She'll stay out at the ranch with me."

"Good. I want to dust for prints in the bathroom."

"Did you find anything from the prints you lifted earlier?"

The sheriff's mouth pressed into a thin line. "No. The only prints I came up with were yours, Laurel's and Mal's. Thankfully, Mal came into town shortly after we left here. I ran into her at Mattie's Diner. She came to the office and let me capture her prints so I could rule her out. Beyond that, nothing."

"So, he's good at hiding his tracks and probably wore gloves." Rage burned in Devin's chest. The guy had to be sick to want to hurt Laurel. Everyone loved her. Especially Devin. She was his only living relative.

"I'll want to talk to her tomorrow," the sheriff said. "There has to be someone, somewhere who has a grudge against her. She needs to think about any interactions with people she's had that might've stirred up anger or been misconstrued. Have her think about men who might've asked her out that she turned down. Hell, maybe she delivered flowers to the wrong person and got them in trouble." The sheriff shook his head. "Hell, even the most innocuous slight she can think of. You never know what will set off some people."

"I'll get her thinking about it tomorrow. Tonight, she might just need to rest." Devin looked around the bathroom bathed in his sister's blood.

"I'll stop by the ranch tomorrow."

"I don't think you'll need to come to the ranch," Devin said. "Knowing Laurel, she'll want to be at her shop, even if she can't use her injured hand to make the arrangements."

Faulkner gave Devin a crooked grin. "You're right. She's always there, rain or shine."

"A little cut on her hand won't keep her down." Devin's lips turned up at the corners. She'd been through a lot worse than a cut on her hand when the Taliban had captured her. She didn't deserve to be targeted again by anyone, let alone her own countryman. "Let's hope we find the bastard before he does anything else to hurt my sister."

Devin left Sheriff Faulkner in the bathroom. As he passed through Laurel's bedroom, he remembered to grab underwear, shirts and jeans from Laurel's dresser and closet. He stuffed them into a gym bag, along with a pair of sneakers. After adding a hairbrush to the bag, he hurried out the door and down the steps to his truck.

As he reached for the door handle, a ripple of awareness slid down his spine. He turned left and right, searching the shadows beneath the store awnings and in the alley. It felt like someone was watching him.

He spun to look across Main Street. The stores were all closed, the lights extinguished inside. The corner streetlights shone down in yellow circles around the base of their poles. Nothing moved except for the occasional car or truck passing by.

Devin glanced up to the rooftops, looking for enemy snipers like he'd done when deployed to Syria and other war-torn countries. Though he reminded himself he wasn't in Syria anymore, it didn't matter. Old habits died hard and might still keep him alive.

He wished he had his night vision goggles. Maybe Jake had some he could use. He'd ask when he saw him at the clinic. If someone were watching him, he could easily lose himself in the shadows of a number of buildings.

Devin didn't have time to search every alley. He needed to get to the clinic and make certain Laurel was safe and taken care of by the medical staff.

He climbed into his truck and tossed the gym bag on the passenger seat. After looking both ways, he backed out of his parking space and headed for the clinic. It wasn't far, and soon, he was parking next to Jake's pickup in the parking lot. He grabbed the gym bag and headed for the door.

Once inside the building, he went straight to the reception desk and asked to see Laurel Layne.

The gray-haired receptionist smiled up at him. "She's popular tonight. We normally don't let more than two people back at a time, but it's been a slow night. I'm sure the staff won't be too bent out of shape over four." She opened a door marked Authorized Personnel Only and told him the room number. "Take a right at the end of the hall. It's the second door on the right."

Devin could hear Jake's voice as he rounded the corner. A feminine voice made Devin's feet slow, and his pulse speed up.

When he turned into Laurel's room, Jake stood at the door, partially blocking his view. Laurel sat on the side of the bed in a hospital gown, her hand swathed in bandages. On one side of her bed stood her assistant, Brandy.

When Jake moved aside to let Devin in, he saw the owner of the voice that made his pulse beat faster.

Mal leaned against the wall, wearing jeans, a blue chambray shirt and worn boots. Her hair was pulled back in a loose ponytail, and she had a few hay leaves clinging to some of the strands. Even dirty from working at the Lucky Star Ranch, she was still the most beautiful woman he'd ever known. His heart ached with the amount of love he still had for her.

When her gaze met his, her eyes flared, and her cheeks flushed a soft pink. She pushed away from the wall and shoved her hands into her pockets.

Devin dragged his gaze from Mal and focused on his sister. "Hey, kid. You didn't have to go to such lengths to get my attention." He moved forward and laid the gym bag on the end of the bed.

"You know me. I love all the drama." Laurel's lips quirked upward as she looked around the room. "We have enough people here to throw a party. All we need is beer."

A woman in a white coat stepped around Devin. "Miss Layne, if you're feeling up to it and have someone to drive for you, we can discharge you."

Laurel laughed. "I think I have a few volunteers.

And I'm more than ready to go now that my clothes have arrived. I wasn't excited about walking out of here in this hospital gown."

"What? You don't like our fashion choices?" The doctor shook her head. "No accounting for taste." She outlined the discharge instructions and had Devin sign that he'd received them and understood what had to be done. "You can leave when you're ready. I caution you to keep your hands off razorblades in the future. You were lucky, this time, that you only needed stitches."

Laurel snorted. "Trust me, Doc, I'm done with loofahs." The smile she flashed toward the doctor was a little tighter than usual. Her face was paler than normal, and dark shadows lay like bruises beneath her eyes.

The doctor turned to the men in the room. "Give the lady some room to breathe." Then she turned to the women. "She'll need some help dressing."

Mal stepped forward and smiled at Laurel. "I've got you covered."

"Good." The doctor handed the discharge sheet to Devin. "You're free to go. Keep hydrated to help replenish your blood supply and don't run any marathons anytime soon." She nodded toward everyone and left the room.

"If you don't need me," Brandy said, "I should head home and rescue my husband from my children."

Laurel reached out her uninjured hand and captured Brandy's. "Thank you for coming to my rescue."

Brandy squeezed her hand. "I'm just glad I heard you scream." She drew in a deep breath and let it out slowly. "I think I lost a couple of years off my life running up the stairs to your apartment. If you hadn't given me a key today, I don't know what I would've done."

"You were amazing. I hope I didn't bleed all over your car."

Brandy patted her hand. "I'm not worried. I've cleaned up worse spills from my kids. And don't worry about coming into the shop tomorrow. I've got it covered."

"Oh, I'll be in tomorrow. We have the arrangements to make for the casino."

Brandy shook her head. "Honey, you won't be making any arrangements for a while. You need to let your hand heal."

Laurel held up her good hand. "I can manage with one hand. Besides, I can watch the shop while you deliver."

When Brandy started to argue, Devin held up a hand. "You might as well save your breath. My sister may seem all optimism and sunshine, but she has a stubborn streak that doesn't know when to quit. She'll be in the shop tomorrow." He turned a stern look on his sister. "But you won't use the injured hand for anything."

She raised her bandaged right hand in a mock salute. "Yes, sir."

After Brandy left, Mal waved her hands at the men. "Get out so our patient can dress."

Devin followed Jake out of the room, pulling the door closed behind them.

"Your sister is amazing," Jake said. "What did you learn from the sheriff?"

"Nothing. The prints he lifted earlier were mine, Laurel's and Mal's. No one else's."

"So, our guy was careful not to leave his finger-prints or anything else for us to go on." Jake shook his head. "I'd get Swede to do some digging, but we don't know where to start. Maybe one of the other businesses nearby has cameras outside their estab-lishments. We might want to see if their systems have Laurel's Florals in their range. She won't be staying there by herself, will she?"

"She's going to stay at my place until we figure this out," Devin said.

"Perfect," Jake said. "As with most of our new hires into the Brotherhood, your first assignment has found you."

Devin frowned. "What do you mean?"

"Your first assignment as a Brotherhood Protector is to protect Fool's Gold's number one florist."

"I don't need to be paid to do that," Devin said. "She's my sister. I'd do it anyway."

"It's kind of how things happen in the Brotherhood. You're going to be paid no matter what. Since your sister needs protection, and you're available, Hank will insist on this being your first assignment. Your initiation into the job. Besides, who better to protect her than someone who cares?" Jake held up a hand to stop Devin from protesting. "Let me ask you this—would you trust anyone else to do the job?" He cocked an eyebrow and waited for Devin's response.

Devin shook his head. "No."

"Let us know if you need help. I'll have our tech support company install that surveillance system around Laurel's building. You can work with the sheriff to look into the video monitoring devices of other businesses. He might already have that on his to-do list." Jake clapped a hand on Devin's back. "I'm headed back to the ranch. If you need anything, let us know. I didn't get a chance to show you what equipment and arms we have available to our team. Hank ensures we have all the latest and best, from radios to tracking devices and Glocks to AR-15s."

"Tracking devices, yes. I'll need at least one of those. As for weapons, I have my own .9-millimeter handgun and assorted rifles we use to take care of unwanted critters. If I need anything bigger, I'll let you know," Devin said. "I could use a set of night vision goggles if you have some."

"I'll send someone over tomorrow with the tracking devices and goggles. How many trackers do you want?"

"Send two." In his head, he told himself he needed one and a spare in case the first one was faulty. In the back of his mind, he knew it was a lie. If the same bastard terrorizing his sister came after any other female, namely Mal, he'd want to tag her with the spare.

"I'm headed home," Jake said. "You know where to find me if you need further assistance. Call day or night."

"Thanks," Devin said. "For everything."

After Jake left, an aide arrived with a wheelchair. At the same time, the door to Laurel's room opened, and Mal peered out. "Oh good, the wheelchair is here." She stepped back into the room and slipped her arm around Laurel's waist as she walked through the door and out into the hallway.

It didn't matter how many times he told himself he was doing Mal a favor, Devin still second-guessed his decision to release her from their engagement. She made his heart ache so much that he wished he hadn't given up the painkillers. Not that they would lessen the pain of losing her.

CHAPTER 7

"I CAN WALK BY MYSELF," Laurel insisted. "And I don't need a wheelchair. My hand is hurt, not my legs."

Mal chuckled. "You're not going to win this fight, sweetie."

The aide smiled. "Hospital rules. If you come in for care, you leave in a wheelchair. Saddle up."

Laurel groaned. "Really? Saddle up?" As tired as she was, she still had a smile for the aide. "I know. You're only doing your job." She settled into the chair.

The aide looked at Devin and Mal. "Whoever is driving can bring the vehicle to the door. We'll wait there."

Devin exchanged a brief glance with Mal.

Mal's heart skipped a beat and then pounded hard to catch up.

She gave an almost imperceptible nod indicating

she'd watch out for his sister while he fetched the truck.

"I'll bring the truck around." Devin turned and hurried away.

As soon as he was out of sight, Mal drew in a shaky breath.

Laurel reached up with her good hand. "Hurts to be so near him, doesn't it?"

Mal looked down at her friend. "You're too observant of those around you when you should be concentrating on your own well-being."

Laurel grimaced. "I just hate to see you both in pain."

"And we hate to see you in pain," Mal shot back. "Don't worry about us. We're adults. Things will work out the way they should." And if that meant she and Devin weren't destined to be together...so be it. Her heart sank to the pit of her belly at that thought.

Mal walked at Laurel's side as the aide wheeled the chair toward the exit.

"I think he's second-guessing his decision," Laurel said.

"Ever the optimist," Mal muttered. She wasn't convinced.

They arrived at the exit, and the glass doors slid open. They stepped out into the cool mountain air.

Headlights flashed into their eyes as Devin's truck swung up to the door and stopped. He got out and rounded the front of his vehicle.

Laurel pushed up from the wheelchair and grinned. "See? I can get around on my own."

Almost as soon as the words left her mouth, her eyes rolled back, and she slumped. She would have hit the ground if Devin and Mal hadn't rushed forward and caught her.

Their arms entwined around Laurel, brushing against each other.

A jolt of electricity blasted through Mal's veins. She met Devin's gaze over the top of Laurel's head and couldn't look away. She wanted to be with him so badly, she felt like she lost a part of him when they weren't together. As cliché as it sounded, she wasn't whole without him. He completed her.

"You two can let go of me," Laurel said, breaking through Mal's haze of longing. "I can stand on my own. I just wanted to see if you two were paying attention."

Mal dragged her gaze away from Devin and slowly backed away, lowering her arms to her side. "Seriously?"

Laurel blushed. "Well, what else could I do? You both look like a couple of lovesick deer on opposite sides of a fence of your own making." She shouldered past them and climbed into the truck without their help.

"You little faker," Mal said.

"I'm hungry, tired and the lidocaine is wearing off my hand. Let's get going. And, Mal, I'll need your help at the ranch. You might as well stay the night. I'm not sure I can get in and out of my clothes one-handed. And no, I don't want my brother dressing me. I don't want to scar him for life." She started to reach for the door with her bandaged hand and stopped, her usual smile absent. "It's going to take some getting used to."

Laurel twisted in her seat and reached for the door with her left hand, she teetered on the edge of the seat and almost fell out.

Devin climbed up on the running board, reached in and secured her seatbelt over her lap and then got down, trying not to wince as his feet touched the ground. He closed Laurel's door and turned to face Mal. "I know you'd rather be anywhere but near me, but Laurel's right. She needs a woman to help her in and out of her clothes."

Mal nodded. It would be hard to be under the same roof as the man she loved with all her heart and not touch or hold him. She wouldn't let Laurel down by refusing to help. "I'll take my own truck. First, I want to stop by my place and grab some clothes and my toothbrush. I'll be a few minutes behind you."

Devin held her gaze for a moment longer. "Thank you." Then he rounded the front of the truck, climbed into the driver's seat and drove away.

Again, Mal had to remind herself to breathe. The man had her so knotted up inside she couldn't think straight. And now, they were destined to spend the night in the same house.

Mal ping-ponged between dread and excitement. How would she keep from making a fool of herself around him? Her strongest urge was to throw herself at his feet and beg him to take her back. Mal had never begged anyone for anything.

Her pride made her work harder than most. She refused to rely on anyone but herself to make it in the world. When she'd agreed to marry Devin, she'd taken the biggest leap of faith she ever had and had allowed someone else to hold sway over her happiness and destiny.

Yes, she could live without Devin.

She didn't want to.

The more she thought about spending the night in Devin's house, the hotter her body burned. Desire built like a flame to tinder under the logs on a bonfire.

Different scenarios tumbled through her head as she drove to her house. What if she showed up at his bedroom door in the white babydoll nightgown she'd purchased to surprise him upon his return to Fool's Gold? Could he resist her?

Or she could show up dressed as she was and unbutton her shirt one button at a time and see if he was the least bit tempted.

Or she could wait until he was asleep, slip into his bed and wake him with a kiss. Of course, she would be naked, and he wouldn't be able to keep his hands off her.

The possibility that he might reject any one of those scenarios where she attempted to seduce him had her breathing erratically and her heart racing like she was having a panic attack.

As soon as she pulled into her driveway, she leaped out of her truck and raced for the front door.

Key in hand, she went to insert it into the lock, only to discover the door was already open. It took a full second for that fact to sink in and only half a second more for her to fly off the porch and beat it back to her truck.

She climbed in, slammed the door shut, locked it and stared at her house with the door hanging slightly open.

"What the hell?" she whispered.

She dove into her glove box for the pistol she kept there while driving around the ranch and found a rattlesnake near the barn or horses. Or when a feral dog wandered too close to some of her newborn calves. She used the gun to scare it off.

Now, she checked the magazine. The last time she'd fired it had been to kill a rattlesnake too close to the henhouse. One bullet was missing from the ten-round magazine. That left nine bullets.

With her gun leading the way, she could enter her house and check for intruders.

Mal shook her head. She'd only ever shot

rattlesnakes and rabid raccoons or skunks. She'd never shot a human. If someone was still in her house, could she pull the trigger?

Mal decided she didn't want to put that question to the test. With her gun ready, her doors locked and the windows up, she fired off a call to 911. Within minutes, a sheriff's SUV drove up into her yard. She hoped the man inside was one of the deputies.

Her hopes were dashed when Sheriff Jim Faulkner stepped out of his vehicle and came around to where she sat in her truck like a frightened girly girl, afraid to go into her own house.

Now she had to face the man who'd admitted he had a thing for her.

Mal started to open her door.

The sheriff shook his head and indicated she should roll down her window. "Stay put. I'll check inside."

"But don't you need backup?"

He removed his pistol from the holster at his side. "If I'm not out in two minutes, call for backup. Better yet, get the hell out of here, then call for backup."

Mal frowned. "I'm not leaving you alone with a serial killer."

"Two minutes," he repeated, then turned and walked toward her house.

Mal glanced down at the time on her phone. "Two minutes."

Jim ducked in through the open door. A moment later, the lights blinked on in the living room.

Somehow, that dispelled some of the feeling of impending doom that was applying pressure to Mal's chest.

One minute down. Her bedroom light blinked on. She wondered if she'd made the bed that morning and if she'd left any dirty clothes lying on the floor of the bathroom.

Thirty seconds until she called 911.

Twenty seconds.

Ten.

Nine.

Eight.

Seven.

"Come on, Jim," she murmured.

Five.

Four.

Three.

Sheriff Faulkner strode around the side of the house, waving a hand. "All clear."

Mal slumped against the steering wheel and let go of the breath she'd been holding.

She dragged in a lungful of air, shoved open her door and dropped to the ground. "No sign of the intruder?"

"He's not in the house." The sheriff's jaw was tight, and his lips were pressed into a thin line. "But he did leave something behind."

"What?" Mal moved toward the house, morbid curiosity propelling her forward.

"You'll have to see for yourself," he said, walking with her up the front porch steps and through the door. "Don't touch anything. I'll have my team go through and dust for prints. But if he's the same guy from Laurel's intrusion, he's careful not to leave prints."

Mal stepped into her living room and stopped, her heart leaping into her throat.

Each cushion on her sofa had been gutted, the stuffing strewn across the room. Her coffee table had been demolished as if someone had jumped on it until it had splintered and collapsed. The glass curio cabinet filled with the little knickknacks she'd collected over the years lay face down on the floor, the glass doors shattered.

The destruction of her furniture was nothing compared to the bold message scrawled across her wall in blood-red paint.

NOTHING YOU CAN DO
WILL SAVE HER

Mal's breath caught in her throat, and gooseflesh rose on her arms. "What does that mean?" she said, barely pushing enough air past her constricted vocal cords to be heard.

"I'm not sure, but since it's in your house, it's a

threat to you or someone you care about. A female someone. My bet is it's about Laurel since she was the one physically attacked by hiding a razor blade in her loofah."

The sheriff pulled his cell phone out of his pocket and snapped pictures of the message on the wall and the destruction in the living room. Then he turned to Mal. "I'm sorry to say, this isn't the only room affected." He gripped her elbow and walked with her into her kitchen, where what looked like the entire contents of her pantry had been dumped on the floor, the shelves had been knocked out and not a single glass or dish remained intact.

She reminded herself that these were just inanimate objects...things. The message on the living room wall was about a living, breathing person.

Mal turned toward the bedroom, fully expecting the bed to be torn apart and the contents of her drawers and closets to be ripped, shredded and slung across the floor.

Instead, she found her bed and dresser intact. The comforter was as she'd left it that morning, slung halfway across the mattress. What was different was the white babydoll nightgown lying across the bed with red paint in the shape of a heart splashed across the left breast. An ornate dagger had been plunged through the middle of the painted heart.

Mal pressed a hand to her chest.

"I know it's hard to see past the messages and

destruction, but do you notice anything that might be missing?"

"I don't own anything worth stealing. I don't even have a television, stereo or electronic tablet. I keep my money in the bank and my gun in my truck." Mal turned to the sheriff. "This isn't a theft. It's a warning." She shook her head. "No. Not a warning. It's a promise. If he's targeting a woman in my life, he plans on killing her."

Sheriff Faulkner approached the nightstand. The drawer hung open a couple of inches. What do you keep in this drawer?"

"Nothing important—" Mal's heart stalled. She hurried forward. "Except for some old letters." Without touching the drawer, she peered inside. The stack of handwritten letters she'd received from Devin was gone. She pressed a hand to her chest to keep her heart from breaking. "My letters."

"What kind of letters?" the sheriff asked.

"Love letters from my fiancé," she whispered, her voice catching in her constricted throat. She looked around the room, bent to glance under the bed and behind the nightstand. "They were bound together with a ribbon."

The sheriff moved around the room as well, searching, careful not to touch anything. Finally, he stepped into the bathroom. A moment later, he called out, "Was it a red ribbon?"

"Yes!" she cried and ran to the bathroom door.

The sheriff stood just inside the doorway. "He dumped your towels and linens on the floor and poured your hair products and cleaning supplies over all of it."

Her towels and sheets lay in a heap in the middle of the room, with every bottle of anything she'd kept stored for hygiene and cleaning spilled over them. The empty bottles lay where they'd been thrown or dropped.

The sheriff stood over her small trashcan. Part of a red ribbon draped over the edge of the can.

"My letters!" Mal cried and dove through the door.

"Sorry." The sheriff shook his head. "Not anymore."

Mal swallowed a sob as she peered into the can. The acrid scent of burned paper filled her nostrils. All that remained of her cherished letters were black and gray ashes. The ribbon's other end was gone. What was left was a small piece of red satin with a burned end.

Those letters had been her lifeline while Devin had been deployed. She'd read each one at least a dozen times, memorizing every word. She dropped to her knees, tears sliding down her cheeks. Losing the letters was one more knife jab to her already hemorrhaging heart. "Why?"

"I don't know." Jim gripped her elbow and helped her to her feet. "Whatever it means, you can't stay here. This place is now a crime scene," Sheriff Faulkner gripped her elbow and led her out of the bathroom and through the bedroom.

Mal dug in her heels. "I need clothes and toiletries before I'm banned from my house."

"Don't get into your dresser. He had to touch the handles to get to that nightgown. Same with the nightstand." Jim walked past the bed, stopped and snapped a photo of the dagger. "That's a fancy dagger. Not something you find in most stores in the US. It might give us a clue about who we're dealing with."

When Jim would have led her outside, she dug in her heels. "What about the shower? We didn't check the shower. Did he hide a razor somewhere in there like he did in Laurel's bathroom? I don't use a loofah. Could he have buried one in my bar of soap?"

"I looked behind the shower curtain. I didn't see a razor anywhere. But I'll have my people go over everything carefully."

Mal glanced around the bedroom, her gaze going to the white gown she'd purchased in anticipation of Devin's joyous return. It looked like it had suffered a painful death, along with her own hope for a future with Devin.

Her place was such a huge mess she couldn't wrap her mind around the amount of effort it would require to restore it to order. She had to remind herself that the things he'd destroyed weren't important. What was important was getting back to Laurel and Devin.

If Laurel was the target, until they found the man behind the threat, Mal couldn't leave her friend alone for even a minute.

"We need to go," the sheriff said softly.

"Damn right, we do," Mal said, her voice hardening. "But not without undergarments."

The sheriff pursed his lips. "I want to let you grab the clothes you need, but I don't want you to risk getting sliced by some hidden sharp object. Can you hold out until tomorrow?"

Mal glanced down at her dirty clothing. "I'll borrow a shirt to sleep in and put what I have on through the wash at Devin's place."

"I'll have my team go through your clothing first and have them bring your things out to Devin's place. You might consider staying there indefinitely. You can't live by yourself until we catch whoever's doing this."

Mal considered herself an independent woman. Someone who could live alone and not be afraid. Walking into the disaster that was her house had been a kick in the teeth and a wake-up call. She couldn't stay there. No matter how Devin felt about her, she was going to stay with him and Laurel. With three of them there, they had a better chance of keeping each other safe.

Squaring her shoulders, Mal turned to the sheriff.

"I'm ready to go." She'd leave everything as it was at that moment in time and walk away. When they caught the bastard who was at the center of the drama in both Laurel and Mal's homes, they would put him away and go back to living their normal, happy lives.

Of course, normal and happy were relative. For Mal, happiness hinged on one hard-headed former Green Beret who couldn't see his own value or dare to embrace a future with her.

Mal would have to help him open his eyes. And she would. Like with the horses she trained, Mal didn't give up on the things or people she loved.

CHAPTER 8

MAL HAD PROMISED to be only a few minutes behind Laurel and Devin. When forty-five minutes had passed, Devin got out his cell phone and dialed 911.

"This is Devin Layne. I'd like to speak with Sheriff Faulkner."

"Sheriff Faulkner is out of the office responding to an emergency," the woman manning dispatch informed him.

His grip tightened on his phone. "That emergency wouldn't happen to be at Mal Watt's place, would it?"

"Uh…" the dispatcher paused. "We can't disclose that kind of information over the phone."

"But it can be printed in the newspaper the next day?" Devin muttered a curse under his breath. "Mal is my fiancée. I need to know if she's hurt or in danger. Break the rules, for Pete's sake."

"Word's out that you two broke up. Are you back together? Because I can tell you if she's your fiancée."

"She's my damned fiancée. What's going on?" he demanded.

"She called forty minutes ago about a break-in at her house. The sheriff responded. We haven't heard from him since," the dispatcher said. "If you'll hold, I'll see if I can get him on the radio."

He was placed on hold, listening to horrible elevator music. For the next sixty seconds, he ground his teeth. Patience wasn't his virtue, and he'd run out of it ten seconds in.

"Mr. Layne, are you still there?"

"Yes," he bit out.

"The sheriff is on his way back to the station. Do you want me to have him call you when he arrives?"

"I want to know where my fiancée is. She's not answering her cell phone."

His cell phone vibrated with an incoming call. He held it out and noted the name on the screen.

"Never mind," he told the dispatch. "She's calling now." Ending the call to 911, he answered Mal's. "Where the hell have you been?"

"Nice to know you care," she said. "I've been at my house, wading through what's left of my belongings."

"Jesus, Mal." Devin paced the length of his front porch. "Are you okay?"

"I'm fine. My house…not so much." She told him about her open door when she'd arrived.

131

Devin sank down on the steps and shoved a hand through his hair. "You didn't go in by yourself, did you?" It would be just like Mal to push the limits of her independence and charge into danger. "Please tell me you didn't. No matter how strong you are, you always need a backup, someone who has your six."

She laughed, though the sound was more strained than amused. "I didn't go in. I waited for the sheriff to arrive and check it out first. I stayed in my truck with my trusty .9 millimeter in my lap."

"That's my girl," he said. "I take it the intruder was already gone."

"He was," Mal said.

"Here's something to remember. Some criminals do their thing, like burn down a building or shoot up a church. If they think they can get away without being caught, they circle back and watch what happens next."

"Thanks for creeping me out," she said. "Now, I'll be looking over my shoulder twenty-four seven."

"Where are you now?" he asked.

"Turning off the highway at your gate as we speak," she said.

"Did the sheriff follow you?"

"All the way to the gate," Mal responded. "No. Wait. He's following me up to your house. I told him I would take it from the gate. I'm almost to you. We can continue this conversation in person and tell you what we found."

As the call ended, headlights appeared through the trees as two vehicles wound along the road leading to the ranch house.

"Mal's okay?" Laurel pushed through the screen door and emerged onto the porch.

Devin eased to his feet and stared down at his sister. "What did you hear?"

She held her arm up against her chest. "All of your one-sided conversation. I gather my visitor paid her a visit as well." Laurel shook her head.

Devin nodded. "When she got home, her door was open."

"Jesus." Laurel's eyes widened, and she pressed her good hand to her chest. "She didn't go in, did she?"

"No," Devin said. "She called the sheriff. He went in. The intruder was already gone."

"Thank God." Her gaze went to the two vehicles approaching the ranch house. "Mal and Sheriff Faulkner?"

"Yup," Devin said. "She said they'd fill us in when they get here." He glanced down at Laurel. "Are you up to it?"

She nodded. "Hell, yes. Maybe he slipped up and left behind a clue as to his identity and motivation."

Mal's truck pulled to a stop.

Sheriff Faulkner parked his SUV beside Mal's vehicle.

They both climbed down and approached the porch.

Mal climbed the stairs, shot a brief glance at Devin and held open her arms.

Laurel flung herself into Mal's embrace.

Mal was careful not to crush her injured hand as she held her friend.

"What's happening?" Laurel cried against Mal's shirt.

Mal stroked her friend's hair. "I don't know, but it can't continue."

"What did you find in the house?" Devin asked.

Mal looked to Sheriff Faulkner. "You want to tell them?"

The sheriff nodded and launched into a description of each room and what they'd observed, starting with the destroyed furniture in the living room, leading up to the nightgown with the knife in the painted heart. He showed Devin and Laurel pictures of each room and the closeup of the letters burned in the bathroom trash can.

"Oh, Mal," Laurel slipped her good arm around Mal's waist and hugged her close. "I'm so sorry."

"They were just things," Mal said, her tone flat. Her gaze met the sheriff's.

He gave an almost imperceptible nod. "What concerns me most is the message sprayed in red paint across the living room wall." He brought up that picture.

Everyone leaned close to view it on his cell phone.

Mal repeated the words that had been scrawled across the wall in bold, blood-red paint.

NOTHING YOU CAN DO
WILL SAVE HER

Laurel's face paled. "Who is the *her* he's referring to? You or me?"

Mal's brow furrowed. "At first, I thought it was you because you're my closest female friend. The message is in my living room which, to me, means the *you* he's referring to is me. But now, I'm not so sure."

The sheriff balanced his hands on his hips. "I'm leaning toward both women as the targets. Especially since their homes were vandalized." Faulkner tipped his head toward Mal and then Laurel. Finally, he met Devin's gaze. "Think about it… Both of their places were broken into, one after the other. The movement of the two photographs at Laurel's was deliberate. What or who was the common denominator in the two photos?"

Devin's eyes narrowed. "Me." One had been a photo of Devin's family before his parents had passed. It had been moved across the room. The other was of his engagement to Mal. That one had been left facing down.

"No other women have reported a break-in?" Devin asked the sheriff.

"No," Faulkner answered. "Again…"

Devin nodded. "I'm the common denominator."

"Mal and I are women you love and care about," Laurel said softly. "This feels like someone is targeting us to get to you."

Devin swore and limped the length of the porch and back. "Who has it in for me? I've been in Maryland recovering from wounds. Why not get to me then?"

"You were probably surrounded by medical staff or other patients," Laurel said. "They don't like to leave you alone while you're recovering both physically and mentally."

Devin nodded. A flash of light out of the corner of his eye caught his attention. More headlights appeared on the road leading from the gate to the ranch house.

The sheriff's eyes narrowed. "Expecting company?" His hand went to the gun on his hip.

"No." Devin touched Mal's arm. "You and Laurel might want to wait inside the house."

"No way." Mal stood with her feet braced and her arms crossed over her chest.

Laurel stood beside Mal, her chin held high. "Not without you, Devin."

Devin winced. The last thing he wanted was to feel like he couldn't protect himself or the women he loved.

"We're not weak women who need a man to

protect us 24/7," Laurel said. "We might not have equal physical strength, but we're smart and capable of having each other's backs."

Mal nodded with a quick smile. "What your sister said."

The headlights flashed brightly in their eyes as the vehicle slowed and rolled to a stop in front of the house. When the headlights blinked off, Devin could see a dark truck. The doors opened. The interior lights shined down on the two men inside.

Devin let out the breath he'd been holding. "It's okay. It's Jake Cogburn and Max Thornton from the Brotherhood Protectors."

Thorn grabbed a bag from the backseat and followed Jake to the porch, where they joined Devin, the sheriff, Mal and Laurel.

Jake shook hands with the sheriff and then turned to Devin. "We heard the police scanner mention there'd been a break-in at Mal Watts's place. By the time we were on our way to her house, dispatch had the sheriff following Miss Watts out to her fiancé's place." His lips twitched upward on the corners. "We assumed that meant you."

Devin's cheeks heated. He refused to meet Mal's gaze. Yes, he'd lied about being Mal's fiancé, but he'd done it to get the needed information. With Laurel in his care, he couldn't leave her unprotected to go to Mal. He'd needed to know someone was taking care of Mal. He refused to feel bad about the lie.

Laurel wrapped her arms around herself and shivered. "Could we take the discussion inside? It's getting cold out here."

"Yeah," Mal said. "And if Jake and his bunch could follow the police scanner, so could others." She tipped her head toward the dark line of trees past the glow of the porch lights.

"Right. We're targets standing out here in the light." Devin held the door open for Mal and Laurel.

Jake, Thorn and the sheriff followed them inside.

Devin was last through the door. That feeling of being watched made him glance once more into the darkness.

He turned and locked the door before following the others into the large living room with a river stone fireplace and enough seating for a dozen people.

The sheriff was filling in Jake and Thorn on what they'd found at Mal's house. He showed them the photos of the damage, the message on the wall and the ceremonial knife stabbed through the white nightgown. Both men turned toward Devin as he entered the room.

"The only two women targeted so far are Mal and Laurel," Jake summarized. "Though the message on Mal's wall was a singular *her*, we can't be certain if the intruder is after Mal or Laurel."

"Or both," Thorn added.

"It seems your job has now expanded to protecting Laurel and Mal," Jake said.

"What do you mean, his job?" Mal asked.

"As the newest recruit to the Brotherhood Protectors, Devin has been assigned the task of protecting Laurel from whoever broke into her apartment," Jake explained.

"I'm your first assignment?" Laurel grinned and then frowned. "I can't afford to pay for protection."

Jake shook his head. "We don't require payment from clients who can't afford it." He turned to Mal. "It seems we now need to assign another protector for Miss Watts."

Mal held up her hand. "I can take care of myself."

Devin didn't like where this discussion was going. "I can look out for both women."

"Only if we stay under the same roof 24/7," Mal said. "I work on the Lucky Star Ranch."

Laurel nodded. "And I work at my shop in Fool's Gold. I can't abandon my store because some lunatic is threatening me. I'd lose what I've worked so hard to build."

"And I can't take off work indefinitely while we take stabs in the dark about who this bastard is." Mal shook her head. "We can stay under one roof at night, but all bets are off during the day. I have to work. Bills don't pay themselves."

"Same," Laurel seconded.

Jake clapped his hands together. "Okay, then. I'll

work on getting another one of our team to cover Miss Watts while Devin keeps his sister in his sights. It might take a day to switch things around."

"We'll have to manage in the meantime." Devin wasn't happy about the division of the work. If he had his way, he'd take Mal and Laurel to an undisclosed location and hole up until the perpetrator was caught.

The ladies had made themselves clear. They weren't giving up their jobs to go into hiding. The fact was...he couldn't be in two places at one time.

Devin clenched his hands into tight fists. "The message written on the wall was a death threat. Neither woman is safe."

"I'll look out for Miss Watts until one of my other men free up," Jake said. "I just can't do it until later in the day. I have an appointment with the VA I made six months ago. I won't be free until the afternoon. Can you hold until then?"

"We'll work something out," Devin said.

Mal frowned. "I train horses," she said. "It requires a lot of lunging and riding."

Jake nodded. "Understood."

"And at night, you'll be under one roof here with me," Devin clarified.

"You'll be with me at the shop during the day," Laurel said. "What about the night? You can't watch out for us 24/7. When will you sleep?"

"We have an excellent security system out at the

Lost Valley Ranch," Jake offered. "You're all welcome to come stay there until we resolve the issue."

"I don't want to impose," Laurel said.

"Nor do I," Mal agreed.

"The other option is I can loan you the best alarm system we have," Jake said with a grin. "And he's portable."

"He?" Laurel cocked an eyebrow.

Devin's brow wrinkled. "Portable?"

"My wife adopted a retired Military Working Dog. Striker. He's very territorial. I can bring him over tonight. As long as he's inside the house, no one else can get in or want to get in. At the very least, he'll wake you if someone tries to break in."

"Striker would help," Mal said. "I'd be okay with a watchdog."

"Same," Laurel said.

The two women looked at Devin.

His lips twisted into a crooked grin. "It's a good thing I agree with them. I'd be outvoted if I didn't."

Jake pulled out his phone. "I'll let RJ know Striker has a job tonight." He scrolled through numbers on his phone, selected one and called it.

Jake walked away from the others as he spoke to his woman. "Hey, RJ, I need Striker at the Layne Ranch for the night.... That would be great. Have I told you lately that I love you?" He grinned. "I do. I'll see you in a few minutes." Jake ended the call and rejoined the others.

Though Devin had heard Jake's conversation, he waited patiently for his new boss to fill them in on what he'd discussed with RJ.

"RJ is going to bring Striker over for the night," Jake said. "He's well-trained and the best alarm system you can get without investing in a ton of electronics."

Thorn sank onto the edge of one of the sofas in the big living room and pinned Devin with his gaze. "While we're waiting for RJ, we should discuss your past, Devin."

Devin's brow rose. "What do you want to know?"

Thorn sat back and crossed his arms behind his neck. "For one...who the hell you pissed off, and why he feels he needs to terrorize the women in your life?"

Devin shook his head. "Other than being an ass to my physical therapists in Bethesda, I can't remember."

"Do you remember much about your prior missions?" Jake asked. "I know they probably were secret, and you're not supposed to share that kind of information, but if you speak in generalities, you won't be breaking any rules."

Devin snorted. "I'd tell you about them, but the explosion that wrecked my leg also left me with TBI —Traumatic Brain Injury. My last mission isn't much more than a haze."

"There had to be something during your most

recent military assignment that might've impacted someone. Someone who might be so angry with you, he might want to hurt your family and then you."

Devin's eyes narrowed, and his brow descended. He forced his mind back to that day. The haze eased back, and memories trickled in. "I remember we were going after a man who'd killed several aid workers, doctors and nurses who'd come to help civilians in a bombed-out town."

He pinched the bridge of his nose, trying hard to recall the details of the attack. "Our intelligence sources told us where we'd find him and that he'd have people surrounding him." An image of black-garbed ISIS combatants flashed through his memory. Men in black clothing and turbans carrying rifles, grenade launchers and RPGs. His pulse leaped as it had when he'd been in that little town in Syria.

Khaki.

A flash of khaki shirts and pants stood out among the black ISIS uniforms.

Devin glanced up and met Jake's gaze. "I don't know if it means anything, but there were two people there who weren't ISIS soldiers. They dressed in khaki and were there as bodyguards to our target. One male. The other, by her shape and size, female. She appeared to be assigned to the wives."

Jake leaned forward, his gaze intense. "I'm assuming the couple in khaki wasn't ISIS."

"No. They were mercenaries," Devin said, more certain as the memories came back to him.

"What happened to the couple in khaki?" Jake asked.

"I remember zeroing in on our target and pulling the trigger…" He closed his eyes, his memories playing like a movie. "The female in khaki stepped between me and the target. When she went down, all hell broke loose. Next thing I know, there was an RPG aimed at me and…Minz." Devin's heart thundered in his chest like it had when he'd been there… in Syria, his world about to change forever. His friend's life about to end.

A gentle hand touched his shoulder. He opened his eyes and looked up into Mal's blue-eyed gaze. She stood beside him, her brow furrowed.

"I wasn't aiming for her," he said.

"You were doing your job," Mal said.

"Any idea who the khaki couple was?" Jake asked.

Devin shook his head. "No. Our intelligence source only briefed us that our target had hired bodyguards for himself and his wives." His eyes narrowed. The chaos that had ensued after Devin had taken his shot replayed in his mind. Black-clad figures darted left and right; some closed in around their leader. One second an ISIS rebel held the RPG on his shoulder. The next second… "The man in the khaki outfit was the one who fired the RPG at us."

Jake leaned toward Thorn and whispered something into his ear. Thorn nodded, pulled his cell phone out of his pocket and pushed to his feet. He left the living room and stepped out onto the porch.

Devin could barely hear the muted sound of Thorn's voice as he spoke with someone on the cell phone.

Jake's gaze followed the shadowy figure of Thorn walking by the window. "I asked Thorn to get in touch with Hank's computer guy in Montana. I want him to search for names of mercenaries who might've been working for ISIS, the Taliban or other organizations hostile to the US government or military organizations. In particular, I want him to search for any female mercenaries. I'm certain they will be few and far between. We should be able to narrow down the list quickly."

"*If* that information is readily available," Devin said.

"Oh, it's available somewhere," Jake said. "They have to be able to offer their services through some form of communication. Hank's guy, Swede, is a master at hacking into the tightest databases or networks. If there's data out there, he can find it."

"Do you think the mercenary whose female counterpart was killed is looking for retribution?" Mal asked.

Devin met Jake's gaze. "It's possible."

Laurel held her injured hand close to her chest, her forehead wrinkling. "You'd think that in a town the size of Fool's Gold, with a solid network of local gossips, we'd notice someone sneaking around."

"Unfortunately, Fool's Gold isn't just locals. We have people moving in and out of the area all the time," Jake said.

Mal nodded. "We're close enough to Colorado Springs for commuters to make daily trips. Not to mention the tourists who come year-round."

"Exactly," Thorn said. "Spotting a stranger is an everyday occurrence. Catching one sneaking in and out of an apartment or house...could be a little trickier."

"Especially one versed in being invisible and wiping away any evidence that could be linked to him," Devin said. "With very little to go on, we're at his mercy. We have to wait until he makes his next move and hope we catch him in the act."

Laurel glanced down at her injured hand. "And hope the next act isn't even more lethal."

Devin laid his hand over Mal's hand, still resting on his shoulder. "Now that we're aware of the problem, we'll have to be more vigilant."

"If he's trying to get to Devin through the women in his life, he might ultimately target Devin himself," Jake said.

"I hope he does that before he takes any more shots at Laurel and Mal." Devin's hand tightened on Mal's. "I'll take him on. He'll regret ever fucking with the people I care about."

Headlights flashed through the windows as a vehicle approached the ranch house.

"That will be RJ with Striker," Jake said with a smile. "With the dog in the house, you should be able to sleep through the night."

Devin doubted he'd sleep at all. With the two women he loved most at risk because of him, how could he?

He'd never forgive himself if someone killed one or both of them on his watch. Hell, on anyone's watch.

Laurel was the only family he had left. And Mal...

God, he loved that woman. If anything happened to her, he wasn't sure life would be worth living.

CHAPTER 9

After RJ arrived with Striker, she spent thirty minutes familiarizing the retired Military Working Dog with the house and its occupants.

Mal and Laurel had been out to the lodge often enough to be comfortable around the dog and for the animal to be familiar with them.

Devin was the unknown to Striker, and the dog took a moment to warm up to him.

Having grown up around animals, Devin quickly won over the dog. Before long, he had the Belgian Malinois lying at his feet like an old friend.

Mal wasn't surprised. Devin had always been good with animals. It was one of the things she loved about him and something they had in common.

RJ had brought a cushioned bed, bowls and food for Striker and made sure he had water. After she'd taken him all around the interior and the exterior of the house, she scratched behind the dog's ears and told him, "Stay."

Striker sat back on his haunches, his ears back, tail wagging, eager for RJ's next command. He probably hoped she'd motion for him to follow her out to her SUV.

"He should be all right," RJ said. "Just give him a few belly rubs, and he'll settle right in."

Mal hugged RJ. "Thank you. I can bring him home in the morning and pick him up again tomorrow evening."

RJ shook her head. "Laurel might want to keep him with her at the shop. He just needs to be walked a couple of times a day to relieve himself." RJ bent to scratch behind Striker's ear. "Be a good boy, sweetie. I'll be back to get you soon." Her brow twisted.

Mal could tell she didn't like leaving him. She'd grown to love the dog she'd adopted.

"We'll take good care of him," Devin promised.

"And hopefully, he'll take good care of you," Jake said. "Get some rest. I'll check in with you tomorrow." He tossed his keys to Thorn. "I'll ride with RJ."

Thorn followed Jake and RJ out of the yard.

Mal, Devin and Laurel stood in the living room, watching out the window as the headlights disappeared.

Laurel sighed. "Well, I'm calling it a night. I'll have to be up earlier than usual to get to work on time."

She grimaced toward Mal. "Do you mind helping me?"

"Not at all," Mal said. "You'll want to wrap your hand in a plastic bag before you shower."

"While you're doing that, I'll double-check all the locks," Devin said.

"Good," Mal said.

Laurel led the way into the kitchen and pointed to the pantry. "You should be able to find something in there to use."

Mal found a plastic grocery bag and wrapped Laurel's bandaged hand to keep it dry.

"Thank you for staying here with us," Laurel said. "I know it must be uncomfortable being so close to Devin after he called off your engagement."

Mal gave Laurel a crooked smile. "I'll survive. Besides, I can't abandon my best friend when she needs me most."

"I'm hoping that with you under the same roof as my thick-headed brother, he'll come to his senses and realize what a mistake he made."

Mal felt the same. "I'm not going to hold my breath. But I'm glad to be here. I don't think I could stay at my place alone. Not after..." She shook her head. "It's a mess. And I hate to admit that I'm scared. For you, for me and for Devin."

Laurel nodded. "Me, too." She stared at her bandaged and waterproofed hand. "This could've been so much worse. And it was somewhat of a passive attack. Can you imagine? If the guy is a mercenary, he probably has a lot worse ways to hurt us." She shivered.

Mal wrapped her arms around Laurel. The woman probably knew a lot of those ways to hurt people, having been on the receiving end of Taliban torture. She hated that the beautiful soul that was Laurel had experienced so much horror. And now to be threatened again... "You have us. We'll make sure no one hurts you again."

Laurel leaned into Mal. "I worry about you and Devin. At least we're together. Maybe there will be safety in numbers."

Mal nodded. After a few more moments, she set Laurel away from her. "Let's get you upstairs and into the shower. You have to be exhausted after everything that's happened today and losing so much blood."

The shadows beneath her friend's eyes seemed darker, but she produced one of her signature smiles anyway. "This will be fun. A one-handed shower should be interesting."

Mal followed Laurel up the stairs to the bedroom she and Laurel had hung out in as teens.

"Oh, good," Laurel said. "Devin brought my bag up. Hopefully, he got enough clothes for a couple of days." She fished in the bag, pulling out the contents one at a time. "I think my shirts will fit you. Sadly, the jeans won't since you're at least four or five inches taller than me. But here." She pulled out a pair of sweatpants. "You can wear these."

"That'll help. I can run my jeans through the wash tonight. Maybe I can get into my house sometime tomorrow and see if there's anything of my wardrobe I can salvage."

"Sounds good."

Mal helped Laurel strip to her underwear and then wrapped a robe around her shoulders. She crossed the hall to the bathroom, turned on the shower, adjusted the heat and laid out a towel.

"I feel like a child who can't do anything for herself," Laurel said.

"It's only for a couple of days, so you don't rip a stitch and start bleeding again. And I don't mind." She backed out of the bathroom. "Yell if you need me. I'm going to see if we can find something to eat."

"Thanks, hon."

Mal pulled the door closed behind her and returned to the bedroom, where she'd left the sweatpants and shirt Laurel had offered. She slipped out of all her clothes and pulled on the shirt and sweats.

She padded barefoot down the stairs and headed for the laundry room.

As she passed the kitchen, she heard Devin's voice speaking softly.

She slowed and peered around the corner.

Devin stood beside the open refrigerator, looking inside with Striker sitting patiently at his feet. "Definitely need to get something besides beer. Man and dog can't survive on beer alone. Right?" He glanced down at Striker.

The dog leaped to his feet and turned toward Mal with a soft *woof!*

Devin's gaze shot to the door where Mal stood.

Her cheeks suffusing with heat, she entered the kitchen with her pile of clothes in her arms. "Do you have anything that needs to be washed? I hate to do such a small load by itself, but I need my jeans for work tomorrow."

"I'm sure I do. If you get the washer started, I'll grab what I have and add it in." He left the kitchen, passing her on his way out, his shoulder brushing hers in the narrow doorway.

Mal's breath caught in her lungs and remained lodged there until he disappeared up the stairs.

Striker trotted across the kitchen and stopped in front of Mal.

"Is it just me who forgets how to breathe around that man?" Mal whispered.

The dog lifted his head and let it drop as if he was nodding in response to her question.

Mal's eyes narrowed. "Sometimes, I think dogs are smarter than humans."

She continued down the hallway to the laundry room and loaded her clothes into the washer. It took a moment for her to work the controls and get the water flowing. She'd just poured detergent into the water when Devin entered the room with a basket half full of his clothes.

She reached for the basket. "Let me do it."

He shook his head. "You're not my maid. I'll do it myself."

Mal shrugged and stepped aside. "I heard you talking to Striker. Do you have anything we can fix for dinner? Or were you serious, and all you have is beer in the refrigerator?" Her lips twitched on the corners.

He finished stuffing his clothes into the washer and closed the lid. "I was serious. Only beer and some cheese in the fridge. But I have bread and cans of soup in the pantry."

"We can manage," she said with a nod. "How do grilled cheese sandwiches and soup sound?"

"Like heaven." He set the basket down on top of the dryer. "I'll make the sandwiches if you want to heat up the soup."

"Deal," she said, tamping down the rush of excitement flaring up inside her. It was just soup and sandwiches, not a marriage proposal or even an invitation for a date.

At least he wasn't shutting her out of the kitchen and making their dinner by himself. She counted his invitation to heat the soup as progress.

He waved a hand toward the hallway. "After you."

Mal entered the kitchen and went straight to the pantry, where she found cans of tomato soup and a loaf of bread. While she laid them on the counter, Devin grabbed a package of cheese from the refrigerator and set it on the counter. Next, he opened a cabinet, brought out a cast iron skillet, set it on the stove and lit the burner beneath it.

"Do you have a can opener?" Mal asked.

Devin fished in a drawer for a manual can opener and handed it to her. Then he reached back into the cabinet, brought a saucepan and laid it on the stove.

Mal opened the two cans, poured the soup into the pan, added water and lit the fire beneath it.

"Can I offer you a beer?" Devin said with a crooked smile that made her heart flutter and her knees wobble.

She nodded mutely, afraid to say anything that might change his seemingly light and easy mood.

He snagged two bottles of beer out of the refrigerator and set them on the counter.

Devin twisted the top of one bottle and handed it to her. Their fingers touched. A shock of electricity shot through her, sending heat throughout her body and downward to coil around her core.

She pulled her hand back and took a sip of the beer, shifting her gaze to the saucepan, afraid he'd see the rush of desire on her face. One of Mal's main faults was that she was too easy to read.

As much as she wanted Devin back in her life for good, she couldn't let him see how desperately in love she was with him. He'd rejected her. She wanted him back because he wanted to be with her, not because he felt sorry for her.

He opened his bottle, took a long swallow and set it back on the Formica.

Mal found a wooden spoon and stirred while Devin slathered butter on the bread, laid slices of cheese between two pieces and laid them in the heated skillet.

Before long, he had three sandwiches lightly browned with cheese oozing out the sides.

Mal laid plates on the counter.

Devin turned off the stove, scooped the sandwiches out of the pan and set them on the plates.

Mal was pouring soup into bowls when Laurel entered the kitchen dressed in shorts and a T-shirt.

"Oh, sweetie," Mal said. "I would have helped."

Laurel grinned. "I managed. It wasn't easy, but as long as I don't have to hook a bra, I can do this on my own." She leaned over the plates of grilled cheese sandwiches and drew in a deep breath. "Wow, those smell like heaven."

"Right?" Devin grinned. "I usually have what's needed to make them, but never remember they're an option."

Laurel turned to the bowls of soup and smiled. "Nothing goes better with grilled cheese sandwiches than hot tomato soup. I feel like I'm eleven years old all over again." She grabbed a plate and carried it to the table in the corner of the kitchen. "Brings me back to the days when life was so much simpler."

Mal carried two soup bowls to the table and set one in front of Laurel. "I call it comfort food. It's easy to cook, and this might sound silly, but it reminds me of my mother's hugs."

Laurel smiled. "It's not silly. And you're right." She sighed. "I miss my folks. Sometimes, I feel all alone in a world full of people."

"Well, you're not." Devin laid a plate in front of Mal and one beside hers.

Mal went back for the other bowl of soup, spoons and her beer.

"Laurel, do you want a beer?" Devin asked.

"I'd better not," she said. "They gave me pain medication at the hospital that made me sleepy. A beer would knock me out before I could finish this wonderful meal. Water is fine if you don't mind."

Devin filled a glass with ice and water, grabbed his bottle of beer and returned to the table.

He set the drinks down and held Mal's chair as she took her seat.

For the first few minutes, no one spoke as they ate the sandwiches and soup.

Striker stretched out on the floor between Laurel and Mal and laid his chin on his paws.

Mal wished she could feel that at ease.

With Devin sitting beside her, she could barely concentrate on the food.

Devin polished off his sandwich and lifted his bowl to drink his soup.

"Devin." Laurel frowned.

"What?" He blinked and set his bowl in front of him.

"That's what spoons are for," Laurel said. "Mom taught you better."

Mal chuckled and lifted her bowl to sip her soup. "I usually pour my soup into a coffee mug. Spoons take too long."

Laurel shook her head and sighed as she tried to spoon her soup with her left hand and failed miserably. "I could use that coffee mug about now."

Mal laughed and leaped to her feet. She hurried to the cabinet where she'd seen mugs and returned with one. She poured the soup into the mug and handed it to Laurel.

Laurel sighed and sipped the soup, a smile crossing her face. "I'm rethinking this whole spoon thing. This is so much better."

They finished their meal while talking about people they all knew from when they were growing up and where they were now.

Mal avoided mentioning what had happened that day. It was bad enough that it had happened, and she figured it was on their minds even if they weren't talking about it. If they rehashed the events, no one would get any sleep.

Laurel made it halfway through her grilled cheese

sandwich and finished her soup before she sat back in her chair, smothering a yawn with her bandaged hand. "I'm going to bed."

"Let me help you," Mal said.

"I'd say I don't need help, but I'm so tired, I don't think I can get the cap off the toothpaste." Her eyelids drooped. "And I'd really like to put my hair up in a ponytail before I crawl into bed."

"I can help with both." Mal carried her empty plate to the sink and came back to help Laurel to her feet.

"I know I'll be better in the morning when I've had a good night's sleep and the pain meds are completely out of my system." Laurel yawned. "I just can't keep my eyes open now."

"Come on." Mal hooked her arm with Laurel's and walked with her to the stairs and up to the bathroom. She squeezed toothpaste onto Laurel's toothbrush and turned on the water.

"Mom always kept spare toothbrushes in that bottom drawer," Laurel said. "They're probably still there."

Mal found a toothbrush still in its original packaging and brushed her teeth alongside Laurel. When they were done, they walked across the hallway to Laurel's room, and Mal brushed the tangles out of her friend's hair, then pulled it up into a ponytail on top of her head and secured it with an elastic band.

Laurel slipped into the bed, pulled the blanket up

and laid her injured hand on top. "Thank you, Mal. You can sleep in the room down the hall. It was Devin's when we were growing up. He sleeps in the master bedroom now. Hopefully, it has clean sheets on the bed." She closed her eyes. "I'd help make it, but..." She raised her bandaged hand. "It's a lousy excuse, but it's the only one I have."

"I'll figure it out," Mal said. "You sleep." She turned off the light and started to close the door.

"Mal?" Laurel called out.

"Yeah, sweetie?" Mal paused in the doorframe.

"Could you leave the door open and a light on in the hallway? Ever since they kept me in the hell hole, I'm not so good with closed doors and dark places."

"Sure," Mal said, a lump rising in her throat. This was the first time Laurel had said anything about what she'd endured when she'd been captured and held hostage by the Taliban. "Do you want me to stay with you?"

"Would you?" she whispered. "Just until I go to sleep."

Mal left the door open with light streaming in from the hallway, crossed to the armchair in the corner and scooted it close to the bed. Once she'd settled in the chair, Laurel reached out her good hand.

Mal took it and held it in hers.

"I swear I'm not normally this pathetic," Laurel

murmured. "I've come a long way from the dark place I was. I don't want to go back there."

"You're not going back. Not as long as I'm here," Mal assured her.

"You'll always be the sister of my heart," Laurel whispered.

Mal squeezed her hand. "I love you, Laurel."

"Night, Mal." Laurel's voice faded away.

"Night, sweetie." Mal held Laurel's hand a few minutes after it went limp in hers.

Her steady breathing was Mal's reward for staying until she went to sleep. Knowing that her dear friend was relaxed enough to sleep after what they'd been through that day was a balm to Mal's heart.

Mal rose, tucked Laurel's hand beneath the blankets and slipped out of the room.

Her clothes would be done in the washer and needed to be moved to the dryer, or they wouldn't be ready for her to wear in the morning.

She descended the staircase and hurried to the laundry room where she found the washer empty and the drying going. A smile lifted her lips.

Devin had switched the load.

She ducked into the kitchen and sighed. Devin had cleaned the table and the dishes and had wiped the counters.

Had he gone up to bed?

Mal moved through the house. There was no sign

of Devin or Striker. She stepped out onto the porch. Though the outside light had been turned off, the yard was aglow from the stars shining overhead.

Movement to her left made her turn to find Devin leaning against the porch railing.

"Thank you for being here with Laurel," Devin said softly. "Today had to be hard on her."

Mal moved closer and leaned her back against a post. "I think it brought back some of her memories of her time with the Taliban."

"I'm not surprised. It doesn't take much to trigger someone with PTSD."

He didn't add it, but Mal could almost hear him say, *I know.*

"Did she tell you what happened to her?" Mal asked.

He nodded. "She's a strong woman. Most women wouldn't have survived or would have gone insane."

"She never told me. But tonight, she asked me to leave the door open and the hall light on. She said that ever since they'd put her in the hell hole, she's not good with closed doors and dark places." Mal pressed a hand to her heart. "Jesus, what did they do to her?"

CHAPTER 10

"THEY PUT her into a small hole in the ground, covered it with a metal plate and weighted it down with a huge stone. They'd leave her there without food or water for days. When they finally brought her out, they gave her enough to eat and drink to keep her alive, just to put her back in it again."

Tears filled Mal's eyes. She couldn't reconcile the cheerful, happy, always smiling Laurel with the hostage confined to what amounted to a grave. "How did she get free?"

"The last time they put her into the ground, they didn't move the rock on top of the metal plate. Laurel listened for the sound of rock scraping metal. When it didn't come, she waited until she was sure they'd left, then pushed the plate aside.

"She was weak from hunger and lack of exercise,

but she was able to drag herself out of the hole. She was lucid enough to move the plate back over the hole, knowing they wouldn't be back for a day or so to bring her back up. She hid behind some broken-down trucks until dark. Then she slipped away into the night and walked, following a road to the edge of a village.

"She said she must have passed out. When she woke up, she was in one of the huts being cared for by an Afghan woman. The woman fed her and kept her hidden until she could get word to a US unit operating in an area not far from the village. A Ranger team came in the night and carried her out. They had her medically evacuated to Germany and then home.

"The hell hole wasn't the only torture she endured. They also beat her and raped her a number of times," he said, his voice roughening.

Mal's stomach roiled, and tears ran down her face. "Not our Laurel," she said, her voice cracking on a sob.

He cleared his throat. "I was able to meet up with her in Germany before they shipped her home. Because I was her only family, I was allowed to join her there for the two weeks they kept her there to decompress and stabilize. Then I traveled with her back to Bethesda, Maryland, and got her hooked up with mental health therapists. I couldn't stay. I had to go back to my unit still deployed in Africa at the time.

"I wasn't there when she came home to Fool's Gold. However, I talked with her every chance I could via video calls."

"Then you came home on leave for a month," Mal said.

He nodded. "By then, she'd taken over at the flower shop and was well on her way to a happy life. I can't tell you how relieved I was. She was smiling again and seemed to want everyone to smile with her. Including her big brother." His gaze met hers in the starlight.

"I remember," Mal said. "She was so happy you were home."

"I was glad to be here," he said, his voice low, resonant.

That month he'd been home on leave had been the happiest month of Mal's life. They'd reconnected at the annual rodeo where they'd met years before.

Devin cupped her cheek in his palm and brushed the tears away with his thumb. "It was at that time I ran into my sister's childhood playmate." His lips lifted in a smile. "Only she wasn't a child anymore."

Mal leaned her cheek into his hand and closed her eyes. "You weren't the older teenager I crushed over all those years ago." Mal opened her eyes and stared up into his gaze. "You were bigger, stronger and so damned sexy," she laughed, "you stole my breath away. I couldn't believe you wanted to be with me, the tomboy who would rather wear jeans than a dress and didn't know how to wear makeup. I was more comfortable riding horses than riding shotgun on a date."

"You don't need makeup," he said, brushing his thumb across her cheek again. "You're perfect just the way you are. And nothing is sexier than you, riding like the wind on the back of one of your horses. It's pure grace and beauty."

Her heart swelled with hope. She laid a hand on his chest. "I would have left it all behind and followed you anywhere."

He shook his head. "I was headed back to yet another deployment. You were where you needed to be. I was counting the days until I could get back to you."

Mal moved closer. "We had so many plans."

He nodded. "Finally, my life was falling into place. My sister was recovering; she had a career and business she loved. I'd found a woman who made me want to believe I had a chance for happiness." He lowered his head until his lips hovered over Mal's. "It was everything I'd ever dreamed of."

He was everything she'd ever dreamed of. She wanted him to kiss her so badly.

His body stiffened, and he straightened. "Then my world went to shit."

Mal dug her fingers into his shirt. "But you made it home."

"While others didn't." He drew a deep breath and looked over her shoulder into the darkness. "I came home because I had nowhere else to go—no job, limited mobility and not the man you agreed to marry."

"You're still you," Mal argued. "You're the man I fell in love with."

"We had so many plans for our future. A future involving ranching, raising cattle and children. Hell, I can't keep up with you. You're strong, beautiful and able to run circles around me. I can't even run in a circle. How can I run a ranch with this leg? You'd have to do the bulk of the heavy lifting." He shook his head. "No. I can't saddle you with a crippled husband."

Mal captured his face between her palms. "So, you're willing to let me go to another man? You'll stand back and watch as I marry someone else and have his children?"

His hands gripped her arms. "Yes, I'd let you go. You deserve a better man."

"Do you love me?" Mal demanded, dropping her hands to his chest.

"More than ever. So much so I can't let you sacrifice your happiness to be with me."

"That's a bunch of bullshit. If you want out of the engagement, just say so. You don't have to lie and make it sound like you're sacrificing your happiness for me. Just say you don't love me, and I'll walk out of your life forever. Say it."

She lifted her chin, daring him to say the words that would break her heart into a million pieces.

"Damn it, Mal," Devin said between gritted teeth. His hands rose from her arms to her face. "You know I can't. You know—"

Then his mouth claimed hers in a crushing kiss.

Mal wrapped her arms around his neck and pulled him closer, opening to him.

His tongue swept past her teeth and caressed hers, claiming her in a kiss that ignited the passion Mal knew was there and Devin couldn't deny.

He cupped the back of her head in one hand and slid the other down her back and under her T-shirt.

Her fingers tugged his shirt from the waistband of his jeans and slid across his torso.

The click of toenails on the porch boards barely registered between them.

When a warm, damp nose pushed between them, Mal came up for air and laughed. "Someone is trying to tell us we should be inside."

Striker stared up at them. The fact he wasn't excited or worried about anyone lurking around the ranch house reassured Mal, but they didn't need to tempt fate or their stalker.

She took Devin's hand and led him through the door.

Striker ducked around them and entered the house, going straight for the water bowl.

Devin turned to lock the deadbolt.

When he turned back, he hesitated.

"Oh no, you don't," Mal said. "We're going to finish what we started." She tugged his T-shirt up over his head and flung it across the living room.

"This will only make it harder," he started.

Her lips curled. "That's the idea." She gripped the hem of her shirt and dragged it slowly up her body and over her head, letting it drop at her feet.

With her bra in the dryer, she stood before him naked from the waist up.

His gaze drank her in, his breathing becoming more labored, and he reached for her.

Mal inched backward, just out of his reach. "If you want me, come and get me."

Devin knew he shouldn't give in to his desire. He'd resigned himself to life without her, knowing she was better off with someone else. Not only was his leg messed up, but PTSD was real. He'd woken up too many times punching the enemy only to find he'd been punching his pillow.

"It's not just my leg," he admitted through clenched teeth, struggling to maintain control when he ached to touch her, hold her and make love to her.

Mal frowned. "Are you telling me your injuries include your manhood?"

"Oh, hell no," he said. "I'm hard as a rock." He shook his head. "You see how my sister is…what her experience has done to her. PTSD manifests itself in different ways."

"Enlighten me," she said, bracing her hands on her hips, her breasts jutting forward, beautiful, tempting and making him crazy.

"I have nightmares," he said. "Violent dreams where I wake up swinging."

"So?"

"I would never forgive myself if I hurt you," he said.

She lifted her chin. "I'll take my chances."

Devin's hands clenched into fists. "I can't do that to you. I can't live with you. I'm too dangerous."

She sighed and moved closer. "And I can't live without you." Mal took his hand and carried it to her cheek. "I don't want to argue." She pressed a kiss into his palm. "And I'm not going to bed tonight without you. So, suck it up, buttercup. We're going to rock the springs and twist some sheets. If you want me to leave afterward, I can. If you don't, I'll take my chances. You don't know what will happen. Maybe all you need is a warm body next to you to keep your nightmares at bay."

He stroked his thumb across her cheek. "You don't know what you're getting into."

"Yes, I do. And I'm going in with my eyes wide open." She laid her hand over his and drew it down her neck, over her collarbone, stopping as it reached her left breast. "I'm following my heart. You hold it in your hand. Please. Don't break it."

He sighed, his control slipping away. "I never wanted to break your heart. Right now, I don't have the strength to resist you. I just hope you don't have regrets in the morning."

She smiled. "My only regret will be that the night wasn't long enough."

His hand turned to cup her breast in his palm, and he squeezed gently. "I wasn't kidding about my bad leg. I'm not good on my knees."

Her lips curled. "We'll use our imaginations." She took his hand away from her breast and led him up the stairs. At the top, she paused. "Your old room?"

He shook his head and walked her to the end of the hall to the master bedroom. Once inside, he closed the door and pressed her against it, his hands sliding up her waist to caress her breasts.

"You can't go flaunting them without repercussions." He bent to capture one tip between his teeth and rolled it gently.

"Bring on the repercussions," she said and gasped as his hand slid beneath the elastic band of her sweats.

He cupped her sex and slipped a finger into her slick channel.

"Aren't we a little overdressed for this?" she whispered.

"Yes." He slipped another finger inside her and swirled in her juices.

Her body arched against the door. "Shouldn't we remedy the situation?" she gasped.

"Absolutely." He nibbled the tip of her nipple and flicked it with his tongue, reducing it to a tight little bud.

"I guess I have to take the matter into my own hands." Her hands moved between them, reaching for the button on his jeans. She pushed it through the hole, claimed the zipper tab and lowered it.

Holding onto the waistband of his jeans, she dragged them over his hips and downward, taking his boxer briefs with them. Mal slid down the door until she reached the floor with his jeans.

Devin toed off his boots one at a time and let her push his jeans past his ankles. He stepped out of the denim and shoved them aside.

Mal remained lowered, her hands sliding gently over his scarred leg.

"You don't have to do that," he said, embarrassed by his weakness.

"I know. I'm getting to know the parts of you that have changed." She looked up at him. "It doesn't scare or disgust me. I love every part of you."

Instead of rising to her feet, she adjusted from

squatting to kneeling in front of him, took his cock in her hands and chuckled.

He shook his head. "Woman, don't you know better than to laugh when you have a man's dignity in your hands?"

She grinned. "I was just going to say that I'm glad to see some things haven't changed." She flicked her tongue across the tip of his erection.

His cock jerked in response. He wasn't sure how much he could take before he exploded. It had been too long since they'd last made love.

Mal ran her tongue around the rim and came up to dip into the hole at the center.

Devin's pulse pounded through his veins. He smoothed his hands over her silky hair. When she flicked him again, his fingers twisted into the strands and urged her forward.

Opening her mouth, she took him into her moist warmth.

His breath caught in his lungs, arrested by the strength of his need. He pressed forward, sliding deeper.

Mal gripped his buttocks and pulled him closer, deeper, until he bumped against the back of her throat. She pushed him away until he almost slid free and brought him back in. She repeated the movement in and out, setting the pace and increasing the speed each time.

Devin rocked in and out, the tension building

with each iteration until he teetered on the edge of his release. Holding tightly to his control, he pulled free, grabbed her hand and brought her to her feet. He kissed her hard and fast, then led her to the bed.

She climbed in and moved over to make room for him.

He leaned over her, hooked his fingers into the elastic waistband of her sweatpants and slid them down her legs and off. She lay naked on the bed, her skin smooth and silky, her hair splayed out on the pillow.

"You're even more beautiful than I remembered," he said.

She touched a hand to the tuft of hair over her sex. "Make love to me, Devin."

"That's the plan, but first things first." Devin laid beside her, gripped her hips and rolled her over on top of him. He reached between them, feeling for her sex, frustrated that he couldn't get to it with her body pressed against his.

She chuckled. "Let me help." She climbed off him, turned her back and lifted her leg over his head, planting her knees on either side of his ears. Then she lowered herself over his face.

Devin took her offering by grasping her buttocks and pulling her even closer until his tongue touched her clit.

She sucked in a sharp breath and arched away from him.

He brought her back down and flicked her again.

Mal moaned and sank lower.

He licked her clit several times and thrust his tongue into her slick channel, swirling around, tasting her essence. When he came back to that little nubbin of pleasure, he focused his attention on bringing her to the brink and pushing her over the edge.

Mal braced her hands on either side of Devin's hips. As he teased her center, she took him into her mouth again and sucked him in all the way to the hilt.

He didn't have far to go to his release, but he was determined to get her there first. The more she sucked, the harder it was for him to hold back.

Devin flicked, swirled and sucked on her clit, working it harder and faster with each stroke.

Her body tensed, and she slowed her attack on his cock.

After several more flicks of his tongue, she froze except for her pelvis, which rocked against his mouth in short, sharp bursts as she rode her release all the way to the end. Devin didn't let up until she pulled free of him and pressed her lips to his balls.

"Holy shit," she whispered, her breath warm against his inner thigh. Then she was off him altogether. She spun on her knees and straddled his hips. "I'm so hot and wet; I want you inside me now."

Mal positioned herself over him and used her

hand to guide him into her channel. She sank down on him, taking all of him into her.

He was fully sheathed and on the verge of his own release when he remembered. Devin grabbed her hips and raised her off him.

"What are you doing?" she demanded, trying to lower herself over him again. "We're not done."

"Protection," he said through gritted teeth.

She cursed under her breath. "Where?"

"Drawer." He tipped his head toward the nightstand.

Mal dove into the drawer, found a packet and resumed her position straddled over his hips.

She tore open the packet, pulled out the condom and rolled it over his cock, fondling his balls at the base. Once again, she rose over him, guided him in and sank down. With him buried deep inside her, she leaned over, pressing her breasts to his naked chest and claimed a quick kiss.

Devin couldn't hold out much longer.

When Mal rose on her knees, Devin gripped her hips and brought her down hard. He pushed her up, then brought her down again.

Mal rocked up and down, her back arching while her hand was on her sex, stroking her clit as she rode his cock.

Devin pumped hard and fast until the sensations peaked, and he shot over the edge. He continued to thrust as he rode his release to the end and collapsed back against the bed.

With his cock still throbbing, hard and full inside her, Mal lay over him with a sigh. "Wow," she said.

He chuckled and wrapped his arms around her. "Wow."

She lay for a long time, her breathing slowly returning to normal.

Devin rolled them both onto their sides and pulled her against him.

Her head rested against his shoulder and her hand lay on his chest. "We've still got it, don't we?" she asked.

"Yes, ma'am." He laid his cheek against her hair. "You don't have to stay," he said.

She laughed. "The hell I don't. Every bone and muscle in my body is mush. I'm down for the night. Don't expect me to wake before the alarm." She yawned and snuggled closer. "I love you, Devin," she said.

Devin's arm tightened around her. "Against my better judgment, I love you, too."

Mal's breathing grew slower, and her body relaxed against him. She slept.

Afraid to sleep and slip into one of his violent nightmares, Devin stayed awake into the small hours of the morning when he couldn't keep his eyes open any longer.

He fell into a deep, dreamless sleep.

He slept until a hand on his shoulder shook him awake.

"Devin."

He opened his eyes slowly.

Mal stood beside the bed, holding his handgun.

He sat up instantly. "What's wrong?"

"Striker's barking."

CHAPTER 11

STRIKER'S deep bark had jolted Mal from the best sleep she'd had in a long time. She'd rolled out of bed, careful not to wake Devin, surprised he'd slept through the dog's incessant noise, which was muffled by the closed bedroom door.

Mal had pulled on one of Devin's long T-shirts, the hem covering what was important. She'd found his gun in the drawer of the nightstand next to the condoms, got it out and held it ready.

She hoped Striker was barking only because he had to go outside and relieve himself. Still, she wasn't taking any chances.

Light edged through the blinds on the windows. She glanced at the clock on the nightstand. Six-thirty. Even if Striker wasn't barking, it was time to get up and go to work.

She'd leaned over the bed, wishing she didn't have

to wake the sleeping man. But Striker was still barking. She touched Devin's shoulder. "Devin."

Devin's eyes opened, widened and he sat up straight. "What's wrong?"

"Striker's barking," she said.

Devin swung his legs over the side of the bed and stood. He winced slightly as he strode naked across the floor, yanked shorts out of a drawer and pulled them on.

"I'll take that," he said and relieved her of the gun.

Devin led the way down the hall to the stairs.

Laurel poked her head out the door of her bedroom. She was dressed in a T-shirt and jeans, the button and zipper hanging open. "Couldn't quite get it," she whispered. "What's got Striker worked up?"

"About to find out." Devin started down the stairs.

Mal hurried to Laurel, zipped and buttoned her friend's jeans and then turned to follow Devin.

"I don't remember Striker ever barking like this," Laurel said behind her.

Mal shook her head. "Me either." She hurried to catch up to Devin as he reached the bottom of the stairs.

Striker stood at the door, barking, frantic to get out.

"What's wrong, boy?" Devin spoke softly.

The dog's barking got louder and mixed with deep-throated growls.

Devin crossed to the window and peered around

the edge of the windowsill, his gun in hand. "There's a BMW sports car parked out front," Devin announced.

Laurel laughed. "That will be Alan. He's the only person I know around here with a BMW sports car."

"I don't care if it's a BMW or a VW bug," Devin grumbled. "What the hell's he doing here?"

Laurel pushed past her brother and laid her good hand on the front doorknob.

Devin laid his hand over hers and shook his head. "You two get back. I'll answer the door."

A frown denting her brow, Laurel gave Devin a twisted frown. "Why? It's just Alan. The sheriff ran a background check on him. He's clear. Let him in."

"I don't know why he's here so damned early in the morning," Devin grumbled. He pointed toward the kitchen door. "Go. Get out of here."

Laurel's frown deepened. "But—"

Mal grabbed Laurel's arm. "Let Devin find out what Alan wants."

"I just don't want Devin to get trigger-happy and shoot him." Laurel's nose wrinkled. "I never did like guns, even when I had to carry one in the Army."

Mal chuckled. "Seems kind of weird. Why *did* you join the Army?" she asked as she guided Laurel into the dining room.

"I wanted to travel and see the world." Laurel snorted. "All I saw was the dust and poverty of Afghanistan and its people, some of whom were shooting at us. I did get away from home long enough to realize I came from the best place on the planet—Colorado."

"Stay back from the door," Mal said, moving Laurel around the corner and deeper into the kitchen. Mal didn't follow her own advice. Instead, she peered around the doorframe at the front entrance.

Devin gripped the door handle with one hand and Striker's harness with the other then pulled the door open.

Alan Croft stood in the doorway, dressed in tailored black slacks and a gray polo shirt. He smiled at Devin. "Mr. Layne, I heard your sister was injured yesterday and that she'd be staying at your place."

Devin struggled to keep the dog from lunging at Alan.

Alan frowned at Striker. "Does he bite?"

"Only when he feels threatened," Devin said.

"Well, I don't need to come in. I thought since Laurel's hand was injured, she might need a ride into town."

Devin shook his head. "She doesn't need a ride. She has me."

"Good grief." Laurel brushed past Mal and smiled. "Alan, thank you so much for thinking about me."

Devin and Striker blocked Laurel from passing through the door. Striker barked. In between his bursts, Devin reiterated. "Laurel won't be riding with you. You can leave now. I'm not sure how much longer I can hold this dog's harness."

Alan's brow twisted into a frown. "Are you okay with that, Laurel?"

Laurel frowned at her brother and then smiled. "I'm good with it. And I'll need to be leaving soon," she said, giving Devin a pointed glare.

"If you need a break at the shop," Alan said, "give me a call. I can take you to the diner or bring coffee and food to the shop." He smiled. "Either way, I'd like to see you."

Laurel cast a glance at her brother. "Devin's being a little over-protective. I'll see what I can do."

Alan nodded to Devin and Mal. "I hope everything calms down for you soon." He gave a salute to Laurel. "See you later."

Laurel smiled and waved her bandaged hand. "Later."

Alan turned and left in his BMW sportscar, leaving a plume of dust in his wake.

"You're not going out with that man until we figure out who's doing all this," Devin said.

Laurel's brows dipped. "Alan's okay. Like I said, he doesn't show up in the criminal database."

"Which only means he's never been caught committing a crime," Devin pointed out.

"True," Mal agreed.

"You don't really think Alan could hurt anyone, do you?" Laurel snorted. "The man's a gentleman."

She held up her hands. "Fine. No dating until we figure this thing out. We need to figure it out fast. I'm not getting any younger." Her lips curled into a grin. "And it's really not fair that you two are getting laid and I'm not."

Mal's cheeks turned bright pink. "Laurel."

Devin's lips twitched. "Sorry. The rule still stands. No dating until this thing is resolved. Besides, I'm sure Alan wouldn't want your brother along for the ride as chaperone and bodyguard."

Laurel shook her head. "Don't worry. I'll wait." She walked to the window. "And I was looking forward to riding in his sports car again. Do you think he'd let me drive it?"

Mal laughed. "If he's like most men, he won't want anyone else driving his baby."

"Don't paint all men with the same brush." Devin leaned close and brushed his lips across Mal's. "Do you two have time for breakfast?"

"You don't have anything but cheese and beer in your refrigerator," Mal reminded him. "What did you have in mind?"

"I could whip up some cinnamon toast, or we could stop at the diner and grab a bite."

Laurel shook her head. "I don't have time. I'm already late. I usually get to work by five-thirty, and we have some big orders to fill this morning. I can't leave it all to Brandy."

"How much can you actually help with your hand bandaged?" Mal asked.

"I have one good hand." Laurel held up her uninjured hand. "It's better than nothing." Her lips pressed into a thin line. "I promise not to use the other. I might lose customers if I bleed all over their arrangements."

"We'll ride together," Devin said. "I'll drop Laurel and Striker at the shop and run Mal out to the ranch."

Mal shook her head. "I'm taking my truck. I don't like being stuck without transport."

Devin nodded. "Then I'll follow you out there."

"I really don't need an escort," Mal insisted. "It's broad daylight. I'll be driving on a well-traveled highway. No one is going to attack me in the open. Besides, I'd feel better knowing you'll be taking care of your sister."

Laurel rested her good hand on Striker's head. "I'll have my trusty, four-legged bodyguard to look out for me. And unlike Mal, I'll be with Brandy and surrounded by townspeople. Plus, I'll lock the back door and shove a desk in front of it if that will make you happy." She blinked up at her brother. "You can't be with both of us at once. You have to go with Mal since I'll have Striker."

Mal shook her head.

"I'll be all right," Laurel said with her sunny smile.

"I don't like it," Mal said. "I'd call my boss and tell him I'm not coming in today, but he's out of the country, and the other ranch hands took a full load of cattle to the auction up in Fort Collins late yesterday. They won't be back until after midnight. The horses and other farm animals won't feed themselves."

"Couldn't they go a day without food?" Devin asked.

Mal shook her head. "Even if they could, I have several on medications they get in the morning and the evening. And then there's the bottle-fed calves that are close to being weaned but still require a bottle in the morning and the evening."

Laurel pressed her lips together. "It's settled. Devin's going with you to help you with your chores. You can't be out there alone."

Devin nodded. "Laurel's right. You can't be out there alone. I'll cover you this morning."

"I'll agree on one condition," Mal said. "We call Sheriff Faulkner and get him to stake out the flower shop and watch for any intruders."

"Great idea," Laurel's smile broadened. "See? It'll all work out if we put our minds to it." She raked her gaze over Devin and Mal. "You two might want to put on some pants before we leave. I don't think Fool's Gold or the Lucky Star Ranch is ready for a semi-nude fashion statement." She laughed and winked. "I'll gather Striker's bowls and food while you get ready. I'd like to leave in the next ten minutes."

Mal turned toward the stairs, muttering, "Miss Sunshine rules with an iron hand."

"I heard that," Laurel called out. "Someone has to get this party started."

Mal headed for the laundry room with Devin close behind her.

As soon as they passed through the doorway, Devin kicked the door shut and pulled Mal into his arms. "I don't know where we're going or how this whole situation is going to play out, but you need to hear this…I love you, Mallory Watts. No matter what I say or do that makes you think otherwise, I always will."

Mal pressed a finger to his lips. "Then don't say anything that will make me feel otherwise. And don't push me away out of some thick-headed belief that you're not good enough for me. Maybe I'm not good enough for you." She leaned up on her toes, wrapped her hand around the back of his neck and pressed her lips to his.

He crushed her body against his and claimed her mouth in a kiss that stole her breath away and left her longing to go straight back to bed and make love for the rest of the day.

His hands slid beneath her shirt and cupped her naked ass. "This is what you wear to a fight?"

"What more do I need?" she whispered against his lips.

He pulled her hips closer, his cock pressing hard into her belly.

"Five minutes, or Striker and I will leave without you," Laurel called out from down the hallway.

Mal stared into his eyes, her lips curling on the corners. "Five minutes is all we need, right?" She reached for the hem of her shirt and dragged it over her head. Hooking her thumbs in the waistband of his boxers, she dragged them down until she'd freed his engorged manhood.

Devin groaned. "You tempt me, woman."

She lowered her voice and pressed her breasts to his chest. "Only tempt? You're hard. I'm wet. Two minutes. Max."

He scooped her up by the backs of her thighs, sat her on the edge of the counter and pressed the tip of his cock against her moist entrance. "Two minutes?"

"Max." She wrapped her legs around his waist and tightened her calves around his back, bringing him into her in one swift thrust.

She sucked in her breath, arched her back and moaned. "Yes," she whispered. "Now. Make it hard and fast."

He moved in and out of her, starting out slow and increasing the speed.

"Faster." Mal gripped his butt cheeks and showed him what she wanted.

Devin drove deep again and again, wincing occasionally.

Mal almost told him to stop. His leg had to be hurting. She'd open her mouth to tell him so, but a wave of sensations whipped through her, rendering her speechless. Her channel, like her legs, contracted around him, refusing to let go until they both reached the peak.

Tension built, drawing her body tight like a bowstring being pulled back.

Devin thrust once more, flung back his head and sucked in a breath.

The pure ecstasy reflected in his face launched Mal over the edge. Her body trembled as the fire burned through her to the very tips of her fingers and toes.

His cock pulsed inside her, his seed spilling into her womb.

Mal clung to him until the last wave ebbed. She rested her forehead against his and inhaled a steadying breath.

"Two minutes," Laurel called out.

Mal laughed. "Okay, we took three. I can still dress in less than a minute. Our clothes are in the dryer."

"Our boots are upstairs." He pulled free, grabbed a clean rag from a cabinet and held it under the sink faucet. He handed it to her and let her clean up before rinsing it and applying it to his still-swollen member.

Mal dove into the dryer, fished out her clothes

and handed Devin a pair of jeans and a T-shirt.

After she'd quickly dressed, she leaned up on her toes and pressed her lips to his. "I'll be back with our boots."

"Grab the bag Thorn brought over while you're at it," he called out.

"Will do." She left him to finish dressing and raced past Laurel, who stood in the front entrance, her arms crossed over her chest, her toe tapping against the wood floor.

"Uh-huh," she said. "I know what you were doing in the laundry room, and it wasn't soaking out stains."

Mal didn't slow as she turned and ran up the stairs, a grin wreathing her face. Happiness spread through her like a bright light, filling every cell with sunshine.

She ducked into the bathroom where she'd left her boots after her shower. After she shoved her feet into them, she ran to Devin's bedroom and grabbed his boots and the bag Thorn had brought the night before. She was back down the stairs in less than a minute and met Devin as he arrived at the entrance.

He shrugged into a light jacket and shoved his pistol into the pocket. One eyebrow winged upward. "Ready?"

Mal laughed. "You bet."

"I've been ready," Laurel murmured.

Devin pulled on his boots and then reached into

the bag Thorn had left with them. "You're not ready yet."

"Yes, I am," Laurel said, lifting her chin.

He pulled out a plastic bag marked tracker and opened it. Inside were two necklaces and a device that fit in the palm of his hand.

Mal leaned over his shoulder. "What's that?"

"A tracking device." He held up the necklaces. "And these are what they track." Turning to Laurel, he looped one of the necklaces over her head. "Tuck that inside your shirt and wear it at all times."

She slipped the necklace into her blouse and patted it with her good hand. "Jake has all the cool stuff," she said.

Devin looped the other necklace over Mal's head. "This way, if we get separated for whatever reason, I can find you."

Mal grinned. She liked the idea that he cared enough to want to know where she was. She glanced down at the pendant. "It doesn't look like a tracker. In fact, it's pretty." She lifted it to her lips and pressed a kiss to it. "For luck." Then she tucked it into her blouse and grinned.

Laurel frowned at Mal's smiling face. "I don't think you've stopped smiling since you got up this morning. The sex must have been good."

Mal gasped. "God grief, Laurel. Where's your filter?"

"Gone," she said. "Is this how you see me every day?"

Mal's smile twisted. "What do you mean?"

"Do my grins look as pathetically silly as yours?" she demanded, her eyes wide, expression appalled.

Mal glanced in a mirror hanging on the wall beside the door. Laurel was right. Mal's grin was silly and too broad. It widened. "Yes. You are pathetically silly, grinning at everyone and everything." Mal faced her. "It's what makes you so special. You charm everyone you meet. Keep your silly smile."

Devin touched his sister's uninjured arm and smiled. "Don't change a thing about yourself, Laurel. We love you just the way you are."

"As does everyone in Fool's Gold." Mal nodded toward Devin. "As you can see, your smiles are contagious."

Devin chuckled. "Let's get going. My sister has orders to fill and deliver. Mal has hungry mouths to feed. The sun is shining; the air is neither hot nor cold. It's going to be a beautiful day."

Laurel laughed. "Look at you, being all optimistic."

Mal gathered the dog's things Laurel had collected and started for the door.

Devin preceded them, looking both ways, scanning the shadows for movement. When nothing jumped out, he motioned the women into the truck.

Mal climbed into her truck and followed behind

Devin's. Laurel rode shotgun beside him, and Striker settled into the backseat.

The drive into town went quickly, with Mal immersed in their own thoughts. Despite the dire warning written on Mal's living room wall, she couldn't suppress the happiness bubbling up inside her. Devin was home, they'd made love and her future with him might still happen.

They just had to get past this stalker threat. Then they could sort through their feelings and come to the correct conclusion.

Mal and Devin belonged together.

A frown pulled at Mal's forehead. As wonderful as the night before had been, Devin hadn't whispered any words of commitment into her ears.

Not even while they'd been making love in the laundry room. Then again, it had been spur-of-the-moment, with no time to talk themselves out of it due to common sense or forethought.

Her breath caught in her throat, and her heart hammered against her ribs. She pressed a hand to her flat belly as she realized what they'd just done.

Or rather what they hadn't done.

They hadn't used protection.

She shot a glance toward the truck ahead, wondering if Devin was still smiling. If so, it meant it hadn't dawned on him yet.

On the one hand, Mal would be thrilled to have his baby.

But she wanted him to commit to her because he loved her, not because he felt obligated to provide for a baby they'd created.

Sunshine and shadows warred in Mal's mind as they drove into Fool's Gold.

CHAPTER 12

DEVIN STOPPED at Laurel's Florals and helped his sister out of the truck. When he looked up, Mal stood beside him. He was glad she was going inside with them. He didn't want to leave her alone in the truck in case the attacker made a bold move in daylight.

The shop wasn't open yet to customers, but lights shone from within.

Laurel started to unlock the door.

Her assistant, Brandy, saw her and beat her to it, twisting the lock and swinging the door wide. "Oh, thank God. I was worried when you weren't here at your usual five-thirty in the morning. Not that I would blame you for playing hooky. It's just that I know you. Nothing would keep you away from your business short of being in a coma."

Laurel laughed and hugged Brandy. "We had a late night with more drama."

Brandy's gaze swept her from head to toe. "You're okay?"

Laurel nodded. "I'm fine, except for this." She held up her bandaged hand, then tipped her head toward the people behind her. "Mal's house was vandalized. So, she and I spent the night at Devin's."

"I'm glad you did. I would've worried if you'd stayed upstairs all night," Brandy said.

Striker chose that moment to step forward and sniff Brandy's leg. "Isn't this RJ's dog?"

"Yes. This is Striker," Devin said. "He's going to stay with you two today."

Brandy nodded. "A guard dog, huh?"

Laurel scratched behind the dog's ears. "I like to think of him as an emotional support animal. I'm considering adopting one. I could use the company."

"Get a big one like Striker," Brandy said. "You want one that can make an impression on an intruder."

"I'll look into it," Laurel said. "For now, we have work to do. How's that big order for the casino coming along? I'm here to help as much as a one-handed flower arranger can."

The two women walked to the back workroom, talking about the orders they had lined up and ones that had come in that morning.

Devin's eyes narrowed as he watched his sister step into her role as a business owner. "I worry about her."

"Me, too," Mal said. "When she puts her head down to work, she's not always aware of what's happening around her." She shot a glance toward Devin. "You should stay here. I'll be all right on my own."

He shook his head. "No. Laurel has Striker and Brandy. You don't have any backup. I'm going with you. As well, two people can power through your work faster than one. I just want to do a final check before we go."

Devin walked to the very back of the shop and tested the door lock. It was secure but not the best lock she could have for her store. He made a mental note to swing by the hardware store and buy a new deadbolt to install. He hoped Jake had contacted a company to install the surveillance system. The sooner those cameras were up, the better.

Not feeling overly confident about that back-door lock, he pulled a filing cabinet in front of the door.

"You know that could be considered a fire hazard." Laurel came to stand beside him, staring at the cabinet blocking the back door.

"Just don't have a fire here until I can install a stronger lock." He smiled down at his sister. "I don't like leaving you here."

"I don't like the idea of Mal going out to the Lucky Star Ranch alone." Laurel turned her brother around. "Go. I'll be fine here. There are plenty of people around if I need help. Striker's here should someone try to attack me."

"I'm going. I'll have Sheriff Faulkner keep an eye on the place. Call me if you feel at all weird or uncomfortable." He hugged his sister.

"I love you, Devin. You be careful out there. If someone has it in for you, you'll need to watch your own back."

He nodded. "I'll be careful." He returned to where Mal waited at the front of the store. As they exited, Laurel locked the door behind them. She'd have to open the shop later that morning for customers. Hopefully, Devin and Mal would be back by then.

He followed Mal out to the ranch and dove into her life by helping her feed the animals, administer medicine and fill water troughs.

When she'd done the minimum she could get by with, she looked around and sighed. "I usually exercise the horses and work with the ones in training for the rest of the day, then wrap up by feeding the animals in the evening."

"The exercise and training can wait a day or two," Devin said. "I'd like to get back to Laurel." He slipped his arm around Mal. "Ready?"

She nodded, started toward her truck and stopped.

"What's wrong?" he asked.

She shook her head. "I guess I didn't need my truck after all."

He smiled. "Probably not. Climb into mine, and I'll take you back to Fool's Gold. Until we find this guy, you're stuck with me."

She held out her hand.

He curled his fingers around hers, and they walked toward his truck. Devin held the door as Mal climbed into the passenger seat.

He rounded the front of the truck and pulled himself into the driver's seat.

Mal sat beside him, her gaze on the barn and horses. The job she loved and the animals she worked wonders with.

So much was on hold until they found the guy terrorizing them.

Devin wanted to pull Mal into his arms and hold her until it was all over. He wanted to tell her that everything would be okay. But he wasn't sure it would be. He couldn't be everywhere all the time. The best he could do was to be vigilant and pray he was enough to keep Mal and Laurel safe.

He started the engine and headed back to town.

As they neared Fool's Gold, Mal leaned forward in her seat. "I don't know why, but I have a bad feeling."

"My gut is telling me the same." Devin's foot pressed harder on the accelerator. He didn't slow down until he reached Main Street and was forced to reduce his speed to that of the vehicles ahead of him. He parked in front of Laurel's Florals.

Before he even shifted into park, Mal flung open her door and jumped out.

Devin wasn't far behind her.

With the hour approaching noon, the front door was unlocked for potential customers. Mal blew through the entrance, calling out, "Laurel?"

Devin walked through the door in time to hear his sister's response, "Back here!"

They hurried to the back of the shop to find Laurel behind a huge vase of red and white flowers. With her good hand, she selected a single white carnation from a pile on the table and tucked it into the arrangement. She glanced up with a smile. "I'm glad you're here. I could use an extra pair of hands."

Striker lay on the floor, blocking their path to Laurel.

"Where's Brandy?" Mal asked.

"She's out delivering the big order to the casino. Once she's done there, she has individual orders to deliver. I don't expect her back for a few hours. Meanwhile, I'm limping along with one arm. I'm slow, but I'm getting things done."

"What can I do to help?" Mal asked.

"If you don't mind me giving the orders, I can tell you what flowers to collect and which vases to lay them next to."

"What can I do?" Devin asked.

"I need trash taken out the back door to the waste bin outside." She tipped her head toward the back of the shop. "Brandy and I didn't have much time to move the file cabinet you blocked the door with. We tried briefly, but it was too heavy for us."

"I can do that." Devin gathered the trash, tied the top of the bags and carried them to the back, where he set them down. After he moved the file cabinet, he carried the bags out to the trash bin and tossed them in.

Back in the shop, he locked the back door. The file cabinet wouldn't be necessary as long as he was there, watching over Laurel and Mal. So, he left it where he'd originally found it.

The ladies worked over the flowers for the next forty-five minutes. Devin, who didn't know much about flowers or arrangements, watched the front desk and did his best to answer questions, make sales of premade arrangements and write up orders for the few customers who wandered into the shop. In between customers, he looked around the place, impressed with all Laurel had accomplished. He noticed a piece of wood trim that had worked its way loose on the corner of the counter. Devin retrieved his tool bag from behind the backseat of his pickup. He reattached the trim and went around the shop, looking for other maintenance items that needed to be done.

After changing a few light bulbs and air filters, he assembled a display rack sitting in a box, waiting for Laurel or Brandy to find time to put it together.

His stomach grumbled, and he glanced at the clock on the wall. It was a quarter past one in the afternoon.

"I'm hungry," Laurel announced.

Devin grinned. "I was just about to say something."

Mal pushed a strand of hair behind her ear. "We worked straight through lunch. My stomach is growling. Do you want me to duck into Mattie's diner and bring back some food?"

"You can call ahead and pick it up," Laurel said.

"Right." Mal pulled out her cell phone and was about to dial when the bell over the front door jangled, and Alan Croft stepped in. He carried several bags and smiled.

Striker leaped to his feet and stood with his hackles raised, his lips curled back as he growled menacingly.

Closest to the dog, Mal grabbed his collar. "Sit," she ordered.

Striker hesitated, growling low in his throat.

"Sit," Mal repeated.

The dog sat back on his haunches, his ears pinned back, his eyes narrowed, watching.

Alan stepped closer. "I took a chance that you haven't had time to grab lunch and picked up meals from Mattie's Diner."

"Oh, blessed," Laurel cried and then frowned. "But do you have enough?"

Alan glanced around the room. "I knew you had an assistant, so I brought three. I didn't count on your brother being here, so we're one meal short. You three can have these, and I'll order another."

"That won't be necessary." Laurel stuck the flower she was holding into the arrangement in front of her and wiped her hands on her apron. "Knowing Mattie, the meals are big enough for two people. Mal and I can share one." She turned to Mal. "Can you help me clear this table?" To Devin, she said, "If we could drag the chairs up to the table, we could eat here." She ripped a long sheet of paper off a roll and spread it over the tabletop.

Alan laid out the plastic containers and handed out the packets of utensils.

Laurel sat beside Alan and across from Mal. Devin took the seat beside Mal, facing Alan. He didn't know much about Alan, but Laurel liked him. He'd been out with Mal and the sheriff on that double date. Which still stuck in his craw. He wasn't keen on Alan, who dressed too nicely and was trying too hard. Not that Laurel didn't deserve someone who cared enough to look nice.

Devin just didn't like Alan for Laurel. She could do better.

"I got a variety of different meals," Alan said, smiling at Laurel. "I knew you liked salads with chicken from our date night. I wasn't sure about your assistant, so I picked something—a hamburger and

French fries. And I got my favorite…liver and onions."

Laurel looked across the table at Mal. "Are you up for chicken salad?"

Mal nodded. "I'm good for salad or the hamburger and fries." She held up her hand. "Hard pass on liver and onions."

Alan held up the plastic plate full of salad with pieces of chicken cut up over the top. He set it on the table between Laurel and Mal. "What about you, Mr. Layne?"

"I'm kind of partial to that liver and onions," Devin said. "Since it's your favorite, I'd be happy with the hamburger and fries. Though I'd also be good with ordering another meal from Mattie's."

Laurel had the top off the plate of salad. "Not necessary. You could feed three people on this salad. Besides, I don't need the calories in that burger and fries."

"Me either," Mal said.

Alan set a drink holder on the tabletop. "I got iced tea since I knew Laurel liked it and figured Brandy might like it as well.

Mal looked around. "Do you have cups?"

Laurel pointed to a cabinet below a counter containing a coffeemaker. "Look in the door on the right of the coffeemaker."

Mal rose from her chair and crossed to the cabinet Laurel had indicated. Inside was a package of paper coffee cups. She selected one and returned to the table, pouring half the tea from one of the cups into the paper coffee cup.

Alan lifted his cup full of iced tea. "We need a toast."

Devin lifted his cup of iced tea. Mal and Laurel raised theirs.

"To good food and the people we love," Laurel said and raised her tea.

"Here, here," the others said, raising their cups.

Devin drank deeply and set his cup on the table.

"To the people we love," Alan echoed after the others.

For the next few minutes, they ate in silence.

Striker sat on the floor beside Mal, a low, continuous growl emitting from his throat.

Mal plucked a piece of chicken from the salad and slipped it beneath the table to Striker.

He gingerly took it from her fingers and wolfed it down.

After eating several fries drenched in salt, Devin lifted his tea and drank deeply. He tucked into the hamburger, consuming half before he looked up again.

The ladies had made good progress consuming the salad. Alan ate most of his liver and onions.

Laurel sat back in her chair and yawned. "Mattie makes the best food in all of Fool's Gold." She yawned again. "Now that my belly is full, I'm sleepy."

"I don't think any of us got much sleep last night," Mal said, yawning.

Devin took another bite of his hamburger and glanced toward Mal, his eyes drifting closed.

Striker lay on his side, fast asleep.

"Striker has the right idea," Devin said. "We could all use a nap."

Mal took another bite of her salad and laid down her fork. "I'm done." She crossed her arms on the tabletop and laid her head on them. "I'm just going to rest my eyes for a few minutes."

Laurel chuckled and laid her head on her arms. "Me, too." She winced and adjusted so she wasn't lying on her injured hand. "I don't know why I'm... so...sleepy..."

Devin's head drooped. No matter how hard he tried, he couldn't keep his eyes open. He fought to stay conscious. His gut told him that this wasn't right. He shouldn't be that sleepy. He needed to remain alert to keep an eye on the women.

Across the table, Alan Croft sat up straight, his gaze on Devin. "Go ahead, take a nap. I'll take care of the women."

"No," he murmured. "My job." Too tired to argue, Devin slumped forward, darkness consuming him.

CHAPTER 13

MAL SWAM in and out of consciousness, each time brief and gone before she could form a coherent thought.

The first time she surfaced, someone had hooked his arms around her and was dragging her across a floor. Colorful flowers floated past.

She tried to move her feet to get them under her, but they didn't cooperate. Not that it mattered. She drifted out of her familiar realm all too soon, only to be jolted back to consciousness when her body bounced against a metal floor, her head landing hard.

She lifted heavy eyelids, just barely. Another person lay on her side on the metal floor.

Laurel.

Her world shook as the metal floor shimmied beneath her. Mal was sucked back into the empty abyss, devoid of light and everything else that could give her a clue as to where she was.

She surfaced again briefly as she was flipped upside down over someone's shoulder and carried across uneven ground. What was happening to her? Where was she going? Why couldn't she focus and stay awake?

As she was lowered into a cocoon of hard plastic, her body folded, her knees bent. She laid her head on her arms. Finally, all light disappeared, and she slept.

THE JINGLE of a bell penetrated the haze of lethargy holding Devin hostage to sleep.

A voice sounded from what seemed like far away.

"Devin," the voice called out. "Devin, wake up."

Forcing his eyelids open, Devin stared into a vaguely familiar face. The sheriff? What was he doing in his house? His eyes drifted closed.

A hand on his shoulder shook him. "Devin!"

Again, he opened his eyes. "What?" His voice came out as a whisper.

"Where's Mal and Laurel?"

"Oh, dear," a female voice sounded nearby. "Even Striker is passed out."

A siren sounded nearby. Moments later, the bell rang again. Footsteps clopped against the floor tiles.

Someone lifted one of Devin's eyelids and shined a light into his eyeball.

The bell rang again, and more footsteps sounded.

"Devin," another voice sounded. "We need you to wake up."

He opened his eyes and stared up at Jake Cogburn's face.

"What happened?" he asked, his voice coming out in a rasping croak.

"You were drugged," Jake said. "Where are Mal and Laurel?"

Devin looked around. He wasn't in his house or his bed. Instead, he was surrounded by buckets of flowers.

Laurel's Florals. He and Mal had been helping his sister.

Laurel.

He pushed up on his elbows and realized he'd been lying on the floor. How he'd gotten there, he couldn't remember. When he tried to get to his feet, he fell back.

Jake and the sheriff pulled him upright and helped him into a chair at a table filled with plastic plates of half-eaten food.

"He brought us lunch," Devin said.

"Who brought you lunch?" the sheriff asked.

"Was it Alan Croft?" Jake asked.

Devin nodded, his head still swimming.

"That's not his real name," Jake said. "He's Trent Ryan, prior military, current mercenary. He was in

Syria on your last mission. His partner, Ava Stone, took the bullet meant for your ISIS leader."

Devin scrubbed a hand through his hair. "The bastard drugged us."

"What time did he come in?"

Devin shook his head. "A little after 1:00."

"You've been out for two hours," the sheriff said. "Brandy came back to find you on the floor. Laurel and Mal are missing."

"I put out an APB on Croft," Sheriff Faulkner said, "and I have a couple of deputies canvassing the area for anyone who might have seen someone coming in and out of the shop."

"He had to have taken them out the back," Jake said. "It would be hard to hide the fact that the women were unconscious when he carried them out."

"And he'd need something other than his sports car to carry them in," Faulkner concluded.

"I've got to clear my head." Devin struggled to catch his breath, the horror of the situation squeezing his chest in its giant fist. "We have to find Mal and Laurel. He's already got a head start on us."

Brandy set a cup of steaming coffee in front of Devin. "Drink this. Maybe the caffeine will help."

He sipped the hot brew, praying it would do the trick. Whatever Alan, or Trent, had given them had knocked him out.

Damn. He'd been a fool to trust the man.

The bell over the front door jangled again.

Devin glanced up as one of the sheriff's deputies entered.

Faulkner met him halfway across the shop. They talked in low voices, their conversation barely carrying. The deputy nodded, turned and left the building.

Sheriff Faulkner returned to where Jake stood beside Devin. "A couple of witnesses reported seeing a white van pull into and out of the ally next to the flower shop. My deputy had one of the store owners nearby check his exterior surveillance footage to confirm. Around 1:30 pm, a white van emerged from behind the flower shop and headed west on Main Street."

"Did they get a license plate number?"

The sheriff nodded. "They did. My deputy ran it. It was a van belonging to a company out of Denver. They reported it stolen three days ago."

Jake pulled his cell phone from his pocket and stepped away. Minutes later, he was back. "I contacted a buddy of mine who works with the El Paso County Search and Rescue. They'll get a helicopter up in the air within the next thirty minutes."

Devin shook his head. "If Trent Ryan wanted to make me pay for killing his partner, why didn't he kill me while he had me down?"

"He wants to make you suffer first," Jake said. "What was it he wrote on the wall in Mal's house?"

Devin closed his eyes, the image of the message

replaying in his mind. "Nothing you can do will save her." His heart sank to the pit of his belly. The two women he loved most were in the hands of a sadistic killer who wanted revenge to wreck Devin. "Sweet Jesus."

His cell phone vibrated in his pocket. Devin scrambled to answer it, praying it was Mal and Laurel having escaped the mercenary.

An unknown number flashed across his phone screen.

Devin answered the call. "Where the hell are they?"

Laughter filled his ear. "You'll never find them without me. If you want to find them, meet me at the coordinates I text you. Come alone, or I'll leave, and you'll never see your sister or fiancée ever again. They will die slowly of starvation and madness. Be there." The call ended.

Devin's hand tightened around the cell phone. He wanted to throw it across the room, but it would do him no good. At that point, his phone was the only way Trent could communicate with him.

As Devin's head cleared, he remembered. "I gave Laurel and Mal the tracker necklaces." He pushed to his feet, swayed and steadied himself.

"Where's the hand-held device?" Jake asked.

Devin started for the door. "In the bag in the backseat of my truck."

Jake caught his arm. "I'll get it. You drink the

coffee. You need your head clear if you're going to meet this guy. His mercenary advertisement on the dark web indicated he has combat skills, including sniper accuracy to four hundred meters and experience with explosives."

"Add effective use of mind-numbing drugs to his list of accomplishments," Devin muttered.

Jake left the shop and returned moments later with the tracking device. He had it powered up and was already searching for the two ladies' trackers.

After several minutes of adjusting dials and giving the machine time to warm up, Jake shook his head. "It's not finding them."

"They wouldn't have taken them off willingly," Devin said.

"That's just it. It's not finding the trackers at all, whether or not they're on the women or dropped somewhere else."

Devin took the device and stared down at the screen. "Are you sure the trackers were good?"

Jake nodded. "I checked them myself. The batteries were fully charged. I don't know why they aren't registering on the tracking device. Unless..." His gaze met Devin's. "Something is in the way."

"Like mountains," Devin's chest tightened. "He could've taken them to a cave or into a mine."

"Even with a helicopter in the sky, we might not find them," Jake said. "With a two-hour lead, they could be anywhere. I've transmitted their codes to the chopper pilot. He'll attempt to find them from the air."

Devin clenched his teeth. "I have to meet up with the bastard. He's the only one who knows where they are." His phone chirped, indicating an incoming text. He glanced down at a string of numbers and a note.

One hour. Alone.

Devin applied the coordinates to his map application on his smartphone and swore softly. He barely had time to get there with all the twisting, winding roads between him and the location. "Gotta go," he said and spun on his heels.

Jake grabbed his arm. "Come with me to my truck. No use going out in the boondocks without some protection." He led the way out of the building and stopped beside the back door of his vehicle. He opened the door, flipped up the backseat and stepped back.

A number of weapons and communication devices were neatly arranged in a storage tray, along with an armor-plated vest and helmet.

"How the hell do you and Hank afford all this?" Devin asked as he shrugged out of his jacket and into the armor-plated vest. After adjusting the straps, he slipped his jacket over the vest.

"Not all our cases are pro bono. We've had some high-ranking, wealthy individuals engage us for protection, rescue or extraction."

Devin selected an AR-15 military-grade rifle, two

loaded magazines, a Ka-Bar knife and a scabbard. He clipped the sheath onto his belt and slid the knife in.

Jake handed him the helmet equipped with night vision goggles and a radio. "I'll have a couple of my guys close by with the radio frequency set to the same one and the helicopter close enough without being obvious."

"Just don't get too close, or he might not meet with me. We can't risk angering him. He might decide a meeting to gloat over his success isn't worth the trouble." Devin tucked the helmet under his arm and held out his hand.

"We'll keep our distance," Jake gave Devin's hand a firm shake. "Good luck."

Devin climbed into his truck, glanced down at his phone and followed the directions leading west out of town.

In his rearview mirror, he saw several trucks pull into the parking spaces in front of Laurel's flower shop. The Brotherhood Protectors team would have his back. At a distance. Hopefully, Trent wasn't just luring him out to shoot him. However, his gut told him that was exactly what the man had planned.

He patted the vest. Between the helmet and the vest, he'd be somewhat covered. Running to catch Trent after being shot might prove more of a challenge with his bum leg. It didn't matter. He'd go no matter what.

If there were any chance of Trent telling him where to find the women, he'd go.

The drive to the coordinates took him west of Fool's Gold and up into the mountains on a narrow, twisting road with steep drop-offs and blind curves. Eventually, the road leveled off on a ridge with trees overhanging the strip of pavement, turning daylight into dusk.

As it was, daylight wouldn't last much longer. The sun was well on its way toward the horizon. In this case, the big orange globe would drop below the mountain peaks sooner, plunging Devin into darkness.

He increased his speed, taking curves faster than he should. The sooner he reached the meeting location, the sooner the game started.

That's what this was all about. Trent wanted payback from Devin for killing his partner. He'd orchestrated this game of life and death to elicit the maximum amount of drama and dread in Devin's life.

The closer he got, the more he focused on the mission ahead. He brought his pulse and breathing under control and vowed to get Laurel and Mal back alive. He'd need his wits about him to make that happen. As much as he wanted to go into the fight and kill Trent, he couldn't do that because Trent was the only one who knew where the women were. If he'd hidden them in the mountains, they might not find them until it was too late.

The message written on Mal's wall haunted Devin. He pushed it to the back of his mind, refusing to believe the words written in bold red paint.

He would find them.

Alive.

As he closed in on the coordinates, the canopy of trees opened, exposing a scenic overlook with a small field populated with a few picnic tables. The view of the mountain range was spectacular.

He parked his truck, got out, reached into the backseat to retrieve the AR-15 then secured the helmet onto his head.

"I've arrived at the coordinates," Devin whispered into his mic.

"Roger," Jake's voice responded reassuringly. "We're just a couple of miles back from your location. Any sign of Trent?"

"I appear to be the only one here." His gut told him he wasn't. The tree line was only a hundred meters from the overlook. If Trent was any good, he could make the kill shot from the concealing array of shadows afforded by the tall trees, blocking the sun's late afternoon glow.

He straightened, closed the door to his truck and looked around. One of the picnic tables had something on it.

Devin moved toward the table, his limp more

pronounced. He ignored the pain and kept going. As he neared, he saw a hand-held radio standing on the wooden surface.

"Do you know why you're here?" a voice crackled over the radio in front of Devin.

Devin lifted the radio and pressed the button. "I can guess. You're here to make me pay for the death of Ava Stone."

A long silence followed. "Did Jake Cogburn and his group of special forces has-beens come to that conclusion for you?"

"It was the only reason that made sense. Since your partner took the bullet meant for al-Hassan, you're taking it personally and have come to deliver your form of justice."

"She wasn't just my partner," Trent bit out over the radio. "She was my life."

"I wasn't aiming for her. She was simply collateral damage. I'm sorry for your loss. You both knew the risks of going in as bodyguards for one of the blood-iest terrorists in Syria."

"Ava was my life. My reason for living," Trent said. "And you killed her. For that, you need to feel the same pain."

Devin's heart sputtered, and his chest tightened. "What have you done with Laurel and Mallory?"

"Don't worry. They're alive," Trent said. "For now. I've buried them in fifty-five-gallon drums where no one will find them."

Devin's stomach roiled. The thought of Mal and Laurel stuffed in barrels gutted him.

"They'll die when they run out of air in a couple of hours. Maybe sooner," Trent said. "Nothing you can do will save them, just like when you shot Ava. Nothing I could do would save her. She took her last breath in my arms. Only your loved ones will take their last breaths in a fifty-five-gallon drum. Alone."

"I'm sorry for your loss." Devin's grip tightened on the radio. "But Ava knew the risks. Laurel and Mal didn't sign on as bodyguards to anyone. You know that targeting innocents is wrong."

"Consider them collateral damage," Trent said, his tone deep and flat.

"Tell me where you hid them," Devin said, "and I'll let you live."

Trent chuckled. "You've got it all wrong. You're the one whose number is up today. I'm only humoring you with words so you'll know why and so you'll suffer at least a little while knowing the people you love will die a tragic, slow death, suffocating in a tight, dark place."

Devin's heart ached for Mal and especially Laurel, who'd been through something similar during her captivity with the Taliban. If she made it out alive, she was bound to have more recurring nightmares with this new round of torture.

His fingers tightened on the AR-15.

Trent laughed. "Your weapon won't do you much good when you have no idea which direction to fire."

Devin laid the radio on the table. He locked and loaded a thirty-round magazine into the AR-15 and settled the rifle against his shoulder.

Desperation driving him, Devin aimed toward the shadows and fired, unloading all thirty rounds.

The scent of gunpowder swirled around him, and brass casings littered the ground.

A moment of silence followed. He didn't dare think he'd actually hit the man.

"You missed," came the voice over the radio. "Now, it's your turn."

A shot rang out. The bullet hit Devin square in the chest, knocking the air out of his lungs and sending him staggering backward. His bad leg gave out, and he fell to the ground, jostling his helmet loose. In the fall, he lost his grip on the AR-15. It landed two feet from him.

For a long moment, Devin lay on the ground, fighting for breath and weighing his options. He could roll over, grab the rifle and fire off another magazine full of bullets into the shadows. Or he could play dead and wait to see what Trent would do. Whatever happened needed to occur fast. The women didn't have much time before they ran out of air.

Knowing he couldn't outrun the man, his best option was to let the mercenary come to him.

Moving as little as possible, he slid his hand over the knife hanging on his belt and pulled it free of the scabbard.

Then he laid as still as death and waited. The minutes ticked by. Holding still proved to be as excruciating as moving about on his injured leg. His muscles twitched, aching to move. Devin forced himself to be patient when all he wanted to do was find the bastard and pummel him into the ground.

After what felt like hours, the crunch of gravel heralded someone's approach.

Devin kept his eyelids lowered just enough to appear closed while he peered through his lashes at his adversary's advance. The man carried a high-powered rifle equipped with an expensive scope.

As he neared Devin, he slowed, his eyes narrowing. He nudged Devin's leg with the toe of his boot.

Devin remained still.

When Trent pointed his rifle at Devin's head, Devin sprang into action, sweeping his good leg to the side hard and fast, knocking Trent to the ground.

The man dropped his weapon, rolled over and started to get to his feet.

Devin kicked out again, catching Trent in the face, connecting with his nose. He reeled backward and landed flat on his back.

Blood spurted, and Trent's eyes watered, giving Devin the opportunity to push to a sitting position and then up onto his knees.

Pain shot through him from his injured leg. He powered through it, raising his knife to plunge into Trent's chest.

As his hand came down, Trent's came up, hitting Devin's wrist and knocking the knife loose. It flew through the air, landing in the grass several yards away.

Devin drew on his years of wrestling in high school and soon had the man face down in a headlock, his arm wrapped around Trent's neck, squeezing tightly,

"Where are they?" Devin demanded. He loosened his hold enough to allow Trent a chance to respond.

"I'll never tell," Trent spat out, his voice hoarse.

Devin tightened his hold. "You'll tell me, or you'll die."

Again, Devin loosened his hold enough to allow air past the man's vocal cords.

"Tell me!" Devin shouted.

"No." Trent bucked beneath Devin and rolled over, knocking Devin loose.

Trent lunged to his feet and took off.

Devin reached out, snagged the man's ankle and yanked hard.

Trent pitched forward. His head hit the ground with a loud cracking sound.

The man lay still, his body limp, unmoving.

"Damn," Devin lumbered to his feet, bent over Trent's body and felt for a pulse. There was one, but it was weak. He'd hit a rock, splitting his forehead open. Blood ran down his face.

Devin patted his body, searching for other weapons. In the process, he found a long zip tie curled in his pocket.

Not willing to risk the man regaining consciousness and coming at him again, Devin secured his wrists behind his back, grabbed his knife and rifle and rushed for the helmet.

He slipped it over his head. "Jake, Devin here."

"We were getting worried. What's happening? Did Trent give you the location of the women?"

Desperation washed over Devin. "No, and now, he's unconscious. He's buried Mal and Laurel in fifty-five-gallon drums and sealed them. They don't have much time before they run out of air." His words almost lodged in his throat, and his eyes stung. "Now would be a good time to bring that helicopter over my position. Maybe he hid them somewhere close by."

"Thorn, Cage, Sawyer, Enzo and I are headed your way. We can help search the area. Sheriff Faulkner is on his way with three of his deputies."

Devin didn't have time to wait for them. He half-ran, half-limped toward the tree line where Trent had been hidden. He couldn't have been too deep in the trees, or he wouldn't have had a good line of sight.

After a few minutes of searching, Devin found an

olive-green bag filled with ammunition. He walked deeper into the woods and discovered a four-wheeler.

Moments later, the helicopter rose over the ridge and hovered.

"Tayo here," a voice called out over the radio. "I'm with the Brotherhood. I caught a ride with the rescue team's helicopter out of Colorado Springs airport. As we came up over the ridge, I got a weak signal from one of the trackers."

Devin's heart raced. He hurried out into the open and looked up at the helicopter. "Where?"

"In the valley to the west of your position. I'll send you the exact coordinates."

"Is there a place to land the helicopter?" Devin asked.

"Not at all. It might be an old mining road leading into the valley, mostly overgrown with trees."

"What's the best way to get there fast?"

Tayo laughed. "Nothing fast about it. Looks like a long way by road. You'd have to go almost all the way back to Fool's Gold and come out on a different highway to get to that mining road. It would be quicker to go cross-country, but you can't get your truck down there. On foot might take you as long as by the road."

"Four-wheeler?" Devin spun and hurried into the trees.

"That would work. Do you have one available?"

Devin found the ATV. The key was still in it. He started the engine and drove out into the open as Jake drove up in his pickup, followed by another. Men leaped out and came to stand around Devin on the four-wheeler.

"We heard Tayo," Jake said. "Go. One of us will stay with Trent until the sheriff arrives. The rest of us will come around by the road. You'll need vehicles to bring them home."

Tayo sent him the coordinates. Devin took a moment to orient and then spun around and headed into the trees. Before long, he found an old mining trail leading down the side of the mountain. It was rocky and rough after years of weather eroding the dirt around the boulders.

Devin bumped over the path, holding tightly to the handlebars, pushing the ATV faster than he should, considering the condition of the trail.

At one point, he almost slid off the side of the trail. He goosed the throttle, leaped back up onto the track and continued downward until he reached the valley floor. He didn't bother to look at his watch. He couldn't move any faster. He'd get there when he got there.

After following a trail along a creek bank, he found a low-water crossing. He splashed through and passed beside low-hanging trees where something white was wedged beneath the branches.

The van.

He had to be getting close. When the coordinates indicated he'd arrived, he shut off the engine and looked around, franticly searching for disturbed soil, anything to indicate freshly dug holes.

They might only have minutes before they lost consciousness and slipped away.

"Mal! Laurel!" he called out.

CHAPTER 14

Mal had woken up several times to darkness, her legs cramped, her arms barely able to move. Her head was still fuzzy, and she couldn't get much air. Sleep seemed to be her only option. She drifted in and out.

When she woke again, her mind was clearer, but she couldn't move. She reached in front of her and felt cold, hard plastic. Where was she? Where were Laurel and Devin?

Breathing was difficult, as if there wasn't enough air to fill her lungs. Panic threatened to overtake her. Panic would do no good; it would only use up what was left of the air faster. Forcing her heart to quit racing, she willed herself to be calm and ran her fingers over the hard plastic, reaching up the sides of the curved surface to where the wall ended and some kind of lid, door or top lay flat over her head. She pushed against the lid. It didn't move.

Pushing harder didn't have any effect.

Based on the shape of her prison, she was in a barrel. When she banged her hand against the plastic, it sounded solid, which led her to believe the barrel might be surrounded by something else solid.

Like dirt.

Panic bubbled up, making her heart beat faster and her breathing erratic. No. She couldn't let panic control her. If her barrel was sealed and buried, she only had minutes of air left to breathe. Instinct made her want to draw in deeper breaths to fill her lungs. If she did that, she'd run out of air sooner.

A muffled scream sounded from nearby. "Devin! Mal! Help!"

Laurel. Sweet Jesus. Laurel must be trapped in a barrel as well. Having been captured by the Taliban and suffered a similar torture, she had to be freaking out.

"Laurel!" Mal called out. "Laurel!"

Laurel's screams subsided. "Mal?"

"Yes. It's Mal," she called out.

"What's happening? Where are we? Why can't I breathe?" her muffled voice faded away.

"Alan must have drugged us," Mal said, putting the pieces together. The lunch, the drinks, getting sleepy.

"Devin!" Laurel cried out. "Devin!"

"I don't think he's here," Mal said, praying he wasn't. If he was, he might have run out of air already. Though she doubted Alan could have fit

Devin's big body into a barrel like the one she was in. Would Alan have shot him on the spot?

Her heart sank, and a sob rose to block her throat. Devin couldn't be dead. Not when she'd just gotten him back. She loved that man with all her heart and couldn't imagine life without him.

"I can't breathe," Laurel called out, her voice weaker.

"Don't talk. Conserve what little air you have. Help will come."

"From where? We don't know where we are. Who else will know how to find us?"

"Can you move your lid at all?" Mal asked.

"No," Laurel answered. "It's sealed tight."

"Help will come," Mal tried to assure her when she wasn't sure herself. "Go to sleep. You use less air when you sleep."

"I'm scared," Laurel said.

"I am too, but it won't do us any good to waste the air we have." Mal spoke as calmly as she could when she wanted to scream and rail against their predicament. "The drugs are still in our systems. Let them help you sleep."

"I'm afraid that if I sleep, I won't wake up," Laurel said. "I love you, Mal. If I don't make it, tell Devin I love him, too."

"You're going to make it," Mal said. "Sleep, sweetie."

"This is all my fault," Laurel said. "I shouldn't have trusted Alan."

"It's not your fault," Mal said. "He fooled all of us."

Laurel laughed. "Figures. About the time I think I'm ready to start dating, I hook up with a killer. I don't think I'll ever trust another man."

"There are good ones out there," Mal said. "You just haven't found your person. You will."

"No. I'm done with men. All the good ones are taken. All that are left are the Alans of the world—lying, murdering bastards, who don't care who they take out with them."

"Laurel, stop talking."

"I can't. If I do, I'm dead," Laurel said. "I sat in silence for too long. I can't do it again. Please, stay with me. Talk with me. Don't let me die alone."

"I won't," Mal said. If she ran out of air talking to Laurel, at least she wouldn't let her friend spend her last few minutes alone.

"Do you hear that?" Laurel asked.

"Hear what?"

"An engine." Laurel pounded against her barrel. "Help! Please, help us!"

"Laurel, stop!" Mal commanded. "What if it's Alan?"

Laurel stopped pounding and yelling.

"If he thinks we're gone, he might open the lid to check." Mal willed her heart to slow. "We have to be ready."

"For what?" Laurel asked. "We can't get out without help."

"We have to try," Mal entreated.

The engine noise came closer and then stopped. Silence reigned.

Mal held her breath, praying for a miracle.

Then a voice shouted in the distance, "Mal! Laurel!"

"It's Devin," Laurel called out. "Devin! Oh, Mal. I can't breathe. I'm not going...to...make...it."

"Devin!" Mal yelled, desperation making her heart beat faster. "Devin! We're here! Help us!"

Tears streamed down her face as she yelled. He was alive. Her heart swelled with hope and relief. He's alive.

Her breathing became more labored as she expended the last of her air. She reached up, hit the lid once more and called out, "Devin! We're here!" Only her voice was fading. She tried to drag in a deep breath, but nothing filled her lungs. Her thoughts jumbled and faded, and she became one with the darkness.

DEVIN YELLED several times and then stopped to listen. A soft murmur reached him. He turned toward the sound, walking into the woods. As he went deeper into the trees, the murmurs increased until he could hear voices calling out.

"Devin, we're here." The muffled voice was coming from a small clearing between the trees.

A huge branch lay in the middle of the clearing, lying atop loose soil as if someone had been digging there recently.

"Mal! Laurel!" Devin called out. He grabbed the branch and dragged it away from the disturbed ground. It was heavy and took him precious minutes to move it out of the way.

When he had it far enough away from the disturbed ground, he dropped to his knees and used his fingers to scrape away the soil to reveal the top of a drum. He scraped away the dirt from around the seal and released the lever. The seal remained tight until Devin dug his knife in and pried it loose. The lid came up, and he tossed it to the side.

Laurel lay slumped against the side of the barrel, her eyes closed, not breathing.

Devin reached in, grabbed her beneath her arms and dragged her out of the barrel, laying her on the ground. He bent over her and breathed air into her lungs. Once, twice and on the third breath, she pushed him away and blinked her eyes open.

"Devin!" Laurel flung her arms around his neck. "Mal was right. You found us." As quickly as she'd hugged him, she pushed him away. "Where's Mal?"

"I don't know. Help me find her," he said, desperate to get to her. If Laurel had run out of air, Mal would also be out.

He dug with his hands, searching for the other barrel.

Laurel scrambled to her knees and joined him. In seconds, they found the other top of the barrel, swept the dirt away from the rim and released the seal. Finally, he flung the top to the side and almost cried when he saw Mal. Like Laurel, she lay slumped against the side of the barrel, her eyes closed, not breathing.

He hoped he wasn't too late. With Laurel's help, they dragged her out of the barrel and laid her on the ground. He checked for a pulse.

None.

Immediately, Devin performed CPR—breathing into her lungs and pumping her chest. "Please, Mal. You have to breathe," he said.

"Come on, Mal. It's not your day to die," Laurel cried. "You're stronger than that."

Devin breathed into her again, then leaned close to her ear. "I love you, Mallory Watts. I want to marry you. I can't live without you. Breath, damn it!"

He forced air into her lungs again, and she gasped and then sucked a deep lungful of air. Her eyes opened, and she stared up into Devin's face. "I knew you'd come for us." She wrapped her arms around him and held him close, tears streaming down her cheeks.

Devin held her, his own cheeks wet. He breathed

in the cool mountain air and held the woman he loved more than life.

If she'd still have him, he'd hold onto her for as long as they both should live.

EPILOGUE

MAL STOOD on the wide front porch of the Lost Valley Lodge, Devin's arms around her, happier than she'd ever imagined was possible.

After Jake and his guys had shown up in that valley, he'd insisted they go straight from there to Lost Valley Ranch to debrief and decompress.

Gunny had steaks on the grill, and RJ was busy mixing a huge bowl of potato salad in the kitchen. Mal and Devin had asked if they could help but had been vetoed.

"You two and Laurel need to relax. You had a helluva day," Jake had said.

Yes, they had. And they'd come out alive.

Sheriff Faulkner arrived and joined them on the porch.

"Any word on Alan—Trent Ryan?" Mal asked.

The sheriff nodded. "He'll live to go to trial for three counts of attempted murder."

Laurel sighed. "Good. A man like that needs to be locked up, and the key needs to be thrown away."

Sheriff Faulkner nodded. "He's going to be in jail for a long time."

"It's too bad criminal databases don't have the ability to pick out people with criminal intent," Laurel said. "I hate that I trusted him. I feel like none of this would've happened if I hadn't let him into our lives."

"You can't blame yourself," the sheriff said. "He'd have found another way to get back at your brother."

"That's right," Devin said. "He wasn't going to stop until he'd made me suffer. He didn't care that you and Mal were innocent."

Laurel hugged her brother. "I'm just glad we all made it through, and it's over." She smiled. "I'm going to go help RJ with the potato salad. I can't stand around and do nothing. It gives me too much time to think."

Gunny walked up on the porch with a huge platter of steak, chicken and sausages. "We can all go in and have dinner."

Jake held the door for Gunny and Laurel. The sheriff entered behind them.

Devin held onto Mal when she started to follow. "If you'll still have me, damaged as I am, I want to marry you. I love you, Mal," he whispered in her ear. "I always have."

"And that's all that matters." Mal leaned up and captured his lips. "The rest will come. Job, home... children." On that word, she leaned back and raised an eyebrow, challenging him to disagree.

His eyebrows lowered. "How can I keep up with a child, much less a beautiful wife?"

"You'll figure it out." She smiled up at him. "Just like you've found work. You're a Layne. You land on your feet."

His tentative job was now official. Jake had told him he'd succeeded with his first assignment, proving he could do it and more. "Damn right, I land on my feet—even if I land a little wobbly."

She laughed. "See? You're the same man under all that bullshit you've been dishing out. I love your sense of humor."

"And I love your tough love and patience."

She leaned her cheek against his chest. "Mmm. Patience isn't one of my strong suits."

"And losing isn't easy if I remember correctly."

Mallory winced. "Are you talking about my barrel race or almost losing you?"

He cocked an eyebrow. "It's not like you to knock a barrel over."

"I've never cried over a man before."

He frowned down at her. "You were crying at the rodeo?"

"Look, cowboy. You have free rein on my heart." She poked him in the chest. "Don't make me cry again."

He held up both hands. "I'll do my best not to. It hurts me to hurt you."

Devin gathered her into his arms and held her close.

She loved how she fit perfectly against him, and she loved the way he smelled of the outdoors. Hell, she loved everything about this man, and she'd do anything to prove to him she wasn't making a mistake by choosing him.

"What are you doing Saturday night?" he asked.

"Spending it with you."

He chuckled. "How would you like to get married?"

Her heart skipped several beats and her face split in a smile. "I'm in." She looked up at him, her brow furrowing. "But why the hurry?"

"When you have a good thing going, you don't want to let it get away," he said, pulling her into his arms. "And we have a good thing going."

"We sure do." She grinned up at him. "See? Things will fall into place. Before you know it, we'll have half a dozen kids running around our feet."

"I'd be so lucky." He kissed her and then leaned his forehead against hers. "I'm anxious to get started on that brood."

She laughed. "Could we have dinner first? Gunny's steaks are to die for."

"I can be convinced. But then we're heading back to the house." He leaned back. "Half a dozen kids might take some time."

"I'm willing to put in the effort," she said teasingly. "You're going to make a great daddy."

"And I hope an even better husband." He took her hand. "Let's get that steak. I'm hungry, and steak isn't going to satisfy my appetite."

Mal floated into the lodge on a cloud of happiness. Devin was her man. She was glad he'd come to the same conclusion.

THE END

Interested in more military romance stories?
Subscribe to my newsletter and receive the Military Heroes Box Set
Subscribe Here

ROCKY MOUNTAIN VENOM

BROTHERHOOD PROTECTORS
COLORADO BOOK #11

New York Times & USA Today
Bestselling Author

ELLE JAMES

ROCKY MOUNTAIN VENOM

BROTHERHOOD PROTECTORS

Colorado

New York Times & USA Today Bestselling Author

ELLE JAMES

COMING SOON

ABOUT THE BOOK

VINCENT 'VENOM' Jones, former Navy SEAL sniper, left the Navy after a Taliban kill resulted in collateral damage—the death of a child. Out of the military, and unsure of his future, he's recruited by Hank Patterson and Jake Cogburn of the Brotherhood Protectors. He accepts the position on one condition…he refuses to protect children.

At her former Army buddy's insistence, Maria Elena left her boyfriend, drug cartel boss Diablo, in the Texas border town of El Paso and escaped to Colorado. All she wants is a chance for her and her daughter to start over, free of the cartel and her daughter's abusive father. Only the cartel boss doesn't let go of what he considers his.

When Venom rescues a pretty woman and her child from an attempted kidnapping on his first day in Fool's Gold, he can't turn his back and let someone else protect them. Against his better judgment, he takes the assignment to provide their protection where their lives and his heart are at risk of total destruction.

Preorder Rocky Mountain Venom

DRAKE

IRON HORSE LEGACY BOOK #6

New York Times & USA Today
Bestselling Author

ELLE JAMES

DRAKE

IRON HORSE LEGACY

New York Times & USA Today Bestselling Author

ELLE JAMES

CHAPTER 1

"Damn," Drake Morgan muttered, checked his speedometer and repeated the expletive.

He hadn't realized he'd been going over the sixty-miles-an-hour speed limit until blue lights flashed in his rearview mirror. Lifting his foot off the accelerator, he slowed and eased to the side of the road, just a few miles from his destination.

A county sheriff's SUV pulled to a stop behind him, and a deputy dropped down from the driver's seat.

The tan, short-sleeved uniform shirt stretched taut over full breasts, the shirt-tails tucked into the waistband of dark brown trousers, cinched around a narrow waist with a thick black belt.

Definitely female. Too petite and pretty to be out patrolling the wild roads of rural Montana.

He lowered the window of his Ford F250 pickup,

reached into his glove box for the vehicle registration and insurance information she'd surely request and straightened.

"Sir, place your hands on the window frame," she said.

He raised his hands, one of which held the documents. The other he carefully placed on the window frame of his door, staring out the open window into the barrel of a pistol. He raised his gaze to the deputy's and cocked an eyebrow. "I have a concealed carry license," he warned. "My weapon is in the glove compartment. I'm unarmed at this moment."

"Just keep your hands where I can see them," she said, her tone curt, her eyes narrowed as she held the pistol pointed at his head.

"Can I ask why I was pulled over?" he asked in a calm, even tone, knowing the answer.

"You were exceeding the speed limit," she said. "If that's your title and registration, I'll take those. But no funny business."

"Trust me," he said with a crooked smile. "I've never been accused of being funny."

Her eyebrows pulled together to form a V over her nose as she took the papers he held out for her.

She studied the documents then glanced up. "You're not from around here," she said.

"No, I'm not," he said.

"Do you know how fast you were going?" she asked, all business, no smile.

Drake almost grinned at the seriousness of the young woman's expression and the way she stiffly held herself. "Over the speed limit?"

She snorted. "By at least fifteen miles an hour. In a hurry to get somewhere?"

"I was."

She shook her head, a hint of a smile tugging at the corners of her mouth. "And how's that working out for you?"

"You tell me," he quipped.

She was pretty in a girl-next-door kind of way with light brown hair pulled back in an efficient ponytail.

Drake stared up into her eyes, trying to decide if they were brown, gold or green, finally settling on hazel. To cap it all, she sported a dusting of freckles on her bare face. "You have my information, but let me introduce myself." He stuck out his hand. "Drake Morgan."

Her brow furrowed as she contemplated his extended hand. "I'm Deputy Douglas." She gave a brief nod, ignored his hand and stared past him into the vehicle. "Since you have a gun in the vehicle with you, you'll need to step out of the truck while I run your data."

Already late for the meeting with his team, their new boss, and this his first day on the job, he sighed, pushed open the door and stepped out with his hands held high.

"Turn around, place your hands on the hood of your vehicle and spread your legs," she said in a tone that brooked no argument.

He cocked an eyebrow. "I'm not a convicted felon. I owned up to the gun in my glove box. I'm unarmed and at your mercy."

Having stated her demand once, she held the gun pointed at his chest, unbending, waiting for him to follow through.

Rather than give her a reason to pull the trigger, he turned and complied with her command.

The shuffle of gravel indicated she'd moved closer. A small, capable hand skimmed over his shoulders, down his sides, around to his abs and lower. Bypassing his private parts, her hand traveled the length of his legs, patting both all the way to his ankles.

Out of the corner of his eye, he watched as she balanced her service weapon with her right hand as she frisked him with her left.

Finally, she straightened and stepped back. "Please stand at the rear of your vehicle while I run your plates and license."

He turned and gave her a twisted grin. "Told you I was unarmed."

She backed toward her vehicle then slipped into the driver's seat. Her fingers danced across a computer keyboard as she entered his license and registration data and waited.

Moments later, she got out of her work vehicle, weapon back in the holster on her belt, and strode toward him while writing on an official-looking pad. When she reached him, she ripped off the top sheet and handed it to him. "I'm only giving you a warning this time. Next time, I'll cite you. Slow it down out there. The life you endanger might not be your own."

With that parting comment, she spun on her booted heels and marched back to her vehicle.

"Deputy Douglas," he called out.

As she opened her SUV, she turned to face him, "Yes, Mr. Morgan?"

"You're the first person I've met here. Nice to meet you." He waved the warning ticket. "And thank you."

Her brow furrowed, and she shook her head as she climbed into the vehicle. Moments later, she passed his truck and continued toward the little town of Eagle Rock ahead of him.

Drake slipped into the driver's seat and followed at a more sedate pace. Hell, he was already late. What were a few more minutes? And it wasn't worth getting a full-fledged ticket. He was lucky she'd only issued a warning. She could've hit him hard with a speeding ticket, with the lasting effect of jacking up his insurance rates.

He owed her a coffee or a beer. Since she was the only person from Eagle Rock he knew besides Hank Patterson, he'd kind of like to get to know her better.

It paid to have the law on your side in these back-water towns.

Following the GPS map on his dash, he drove through town and out the other end, turning on the road leading to his destination.

Soon, he saw her, perched on the side of a mountain, her broad porches intact, her late eighteen-hundred charm shining through, despite the need for a good paint job and dry-rot repair.

The Lucky Lady Lodge clung to the side of the mountain, welcoming travelers in search of a quiet getaway in the Crazy Mountains of Montana.

From what Hank had told him, this lodge had been a place for the gold rush miners of the late eighteen hundreds to spend their hard-earned gold on booze and women.

After the gold had dried up, the Lucky Lady had become a speakeasy during the prohibition, with secret passages into the old mine where they'd made moonshine and stored the contraband in the mountain.

Drake had done some research on the old lodge. He'd found stories telling of days when mafia king-pins had come to conduct business while hunting in the hills or fishing in the mountain streams.

Fires had consumed hundreds of acres surrounding the lodge, missing it on more than one occasion by less than a mile. Throughout the years, the lodge stood as she had from the beginning, a little worn around the edges. Recently, she'd been damaged by an explosion in the mine. That's where Drake and his team would come in.

He looked forward to rolling up his sleeves and putting his carpentry skills to work restoring the old girl. He hoped that, like riding a bike, it would all come back to him despite the sixteen years it had been since he'd last lifted a hammer to build or repair anything more than a deck on the house of a friend. The summers he'd spent working on new home construction while in high school gave him skills he wouldn't have known otherwise and the confidence to try new things he'd never done.

Having joined the Navy straight out of high school, he hadn't had much need for carpentry skills. He'd focused all his attention on being the best military guy he could be. That had meant working his ass off and applying for the elite Navy SEALs training.

BUD/S had been the most difficult training he'd ever survived. Once he'd made it through, he'd been deployed on a regular basis to all corners of the world, fighting wars he thought were to help people who couldn't help themselves or protect his own country from the tyranny of others.

Drake snorted. He'd learned all too soon that war wasn't always for just causes. When he'd tired of putting his life on the line for the benefit of big business, he'd said goodbye to what had been the only career he'd ever wanted.

From there, he'd worked with Stone Jacobs as a mercenary in Afghanistan, leaving just in time before the US pulled out and left Stone and the last five members of his team stranded.

Rumor had it that former SEAL, Hank Patterson, had sent a rescue team to get Jacobs and his people out.

Since Afghanistan, Drake had refused to be another hired mercenary. He'd been drifting from one low-paying job to another. Nothing seemed to fit.

When Hank Patterson had called him out of the blue, he'd been working at a small diner in the backwoods of East Texas, dissatisfied with life, unable to fit into the civilian world and ready for any change that would take him away from the diner, the small-minded residents of the town and the meddling mamas bent on matching their single daughters to the only bachelor in town with all of his original teeth.

No, thank you.

Drake had been ready to leave East Texas.

When Hank's call had come, he'd been willing to listen and even come to Montana for a one-on-one chat with his old friend and brother-in-arms.

Hank had offered Drake a job as a Brotherhood Protector, a kind of security firm providing protection, extraction and whatever else was warranted for people who needed the expertise of someone skilled in special operations.

"I'm not interested in mercenary work," Drake had said. "Been there...done that."

"It's not mercenary work," Hank had said. "It's bodyguard, rescue and protective services for real people who need specialized help. We aren't working for big corporations."

Drake had been insistent. "Not interested. Got anything else?"

Hank chuckled. "As a matter of fact, I know someone who needs carpenters for a lodge restoration project. It's good physical work, and the lodge is worth restoring."

"Sounds more my speed," Drake said.

"Come out to Montana. See what we have here and make your decision," Hank had urged.

Drake had remained firm. "I'm not going to change my mind."

"Okay. I get it. But I want you to meet the guys who work with me and get their take on what we do."

"Fair enough," Drake said. "I'd still rather pound nails. It beats slinging bullets."

"I'll put you in touch with Molly McKinnon and Parker Bailey. They are leading the effort to restore the lodge. I've sent several spec ops guys their way already. You probably know some of them or know of them."

"I'm down for some renovation work with a team

full of former spec ops guys, as long as they aren't going to try to talk me into working for your Brotherhood Protectors." He thought he might have insulted Hank. "No offense."

Hank laughed. "None taken. Whichever way you lean in the job front, you'll love Montana and the little town of Eagle Rock."

Anything would be better than the close-minded, stone-faced inhabitants of the small East Texas town he'd worked in for the past six months.

"How soon can you get here?" Hank asked. "The other four SEALs are due to start on Monday morning."

"I'll be there," Drake had assured him.

"Great. See you then," Hank ended the call.

Drake had immediately given the diner his resignation, packed up his few personal items in his furnished apartment and left Texas. He'd driven for two days, stopping only long enough to catch a couple of hours of sleep at a rest area along the way.

When he rolled to a stop in the parking lot in front of the Lucky Lady Lodge, with the Crazy Mountains as a backdrop to the old building, he already felt more at home than he had anywhere else. Maybe it was because he was tired. More likely, he felt that way because he didn't want to move again.

As he stepped down from his pickup, he shrugged off his exhaustion. He could sink his teeth into this project. It beat cleaning years of grease off the diner's floor back in Texas.

With a new sense of purpose, he passed the large roll-on-roll-off trash bin, already half-full of broken boards, crumbled sheets of drywall panels, ruined carpet and damaged furniture. He climbed the steps to the wide veranda and entered through the stately double doors of the lodge.

Six men and a woman stood in the lobby, wearing jeans and T-shirts. They had gathered around a drafting table, all looking down at what appeared to be blueprints.

The woman glanced up. "Oh, good. Drake's here."

The others straightened and turned toward Drake.

As he studied the faces, his heart filled with joy.

He knew Hank from way back at the beginning of his career as a Navy SEAL. Hank had been the experienced SEAL who'd taken him under his wing and shown him the ropes of what it was like beyond BUD/S. Clean-shaven, he had a short haircut, unlike the shaggy look he'd acquired on active duty. The man had a few more wrinkles around his green eyes, but he was the same man who'd been his mentor so many years ago.

Hank stepped forward, holding out his hand. "Morgan, I'm glad you made it. You must've driven all night to get here."

Drake took the man's hand and was pulled into a

bone-crunching hug.

"Good to see you," Hank said.

"Same," Drake said. "It's been a few years."

Hank stepped back. "I believe you know everyone here."

Drake nodded, his lips spreading into a grin.

A man with dark blond hair, blue eyes and a naturally somber expression stepped past Hank and pulled Drake into another powerful hug. "Dude, it's been too long."

"Grimm," Drake clapped his hand on the man's back. "I thought you were still on active duty."

Mike Reaper, or Grimm as he'd been aptly nicknamed, patted his leg. "Took shrapnel to my left leg. It bought me early retirement."

Drake shook his head. "Sorry to hear that."

"I'm not. I was getting too old to play with the young kids. It was time for me to move on." He nodded. "I'm looking forward to getting my hands dirty with something besides gun cleaning oil."

"Move over, Grimm. My turn." A man shoved Grimm to the side. "Bring it in, Morgan."

A black-haired man with shocking blue eyes grabbed Drake by the shoulders and crushed him in a hug. "'Bout time we worked together again," he said. "When did we last?"

"Afghanistan," Drake said when he could breathe again. He grinned at his old teammate from his last tour of duty before leaving the Navy. "We took out that Taliban terrorist who was cutting off heads for fun. How're you doing, Murdock?"

Sean Murdock stood back, smiling. "Better, now that you're here. Thought we were going to be Army puke heavy. We needed some bone frogs to level the playing field." He turned and dragged another man forward. "Remember this guy?"

Drake's brow furrowed. "Utah?"

The handsome man with the auburn hair and blue eyes smirked. "I prefer to go by Pierce. I like to think I've outgrown the Utah moniker."

Murdock laughed and pounded Utah on the back. "You'll never live down Utah. Once an uptight asshole, always an uptight asshole."

Pierce "Utah" Turner's lips pressed together. "Thanks." He held out his hand to Drake. "Good to see you under better circumstances than the last time we worked together."

Drake gripped the man's hand, truly glad to see him. "Taking mortar fire while trying to extract that Marine platoon was not one of our cleanest joint operations. You saved my life that day."

"And you returned the favor five minutes later," Utah said. "I'd call it even."

Drake glanced toward the last man he knew in the group and smiled. "Hey, Judge. You're a sight for sore eyes."

"Didn't think you'd remember me, it's been so long." Joe "Judge" Smith, former Delta Force Operative, was the old man of the group of men Drake would work with at the lodge. Like Hank, he'd influenced Drake when he was a young Navy SEAL fresh out of training. He'd been an integral part of the first joint operation of which Drake had been a part.

He'd hung back to provide cover fire for the team as they'd exited a hot zone. Judge had taken a bullet to his right forearm and had to use his left arm and hand to fire his rifle. The man hadn't missed a beat. He'd held on long enough for the entire team to reach the Black Hawk helicopters waiting at the extraction point.

When Judge hadn't been right behind them loading the aircraft, Drake had jumped out, determined to go back. He'd gone less than twenty yards when Judge had come running, dozens of Taliban soldiers on his heels.

Drake and the rest of his team had provided him cover until he'd dove aboard the helicopter. They'd lifted off under heavy fire and made it back to the Forward Operating Base without losing a single man. He'd made an impression on Drake he would never forget.

"What brings you to Montana?" Drake asked.

"Got tired of wiping the noses of baby Deltas," Judge said. "When I reached my twenty, I figured it was time to leave."

"I always wondered why they called you Judge," Drake admitted.

Judge shrugged.

Grimm laughed. "It came out of a barroom fight. Patterson didn't like the way a man was treating one of the ladies. When he told him to back off, the man asked him what he was going to do if he didn't." Grimm's lips curled. "He became the Judge, jury and executioner."

"You killed the guy?" the woman at the drafting table asked.

Judge shook his head. "No."

"He made him wish he was dead," Grimm said. "He almost got kicked out of Delta Force. If the woman he'd defended hadn't come forward to tell her side of the story, his career would've been over."

Drake glanced around at the men he'd fought with and shook his head. "Had I known we were having a reunion, I would've come sooner."

"I want each of you to know I would hire you in a heartbeat for my organization, Brotherhood Protectors, but you all have expressed your desire to fire nail guns, not Glocks. I haven't given up hope that you'll change your mind, but I respect that you want to try something different. And with that, I'll hand you over to your new bosses. Molly McKinnon and her fiancé, Parker Bailey, are from the Iron Horse Ranch." Hank waved a hand toward the man and the woman who'd remained at the drafting table. "They're the new owners of the Lucky Lady Lodge."

"For better or worse." The man took Drake's

hand. "Welcome aboard. I'm here to do the grunt work, just like you guys." He turned to the woman. "Molly is the brains behind the project."

Molly shook Drake's hand. "Glad to meet you. Now, if we could get started…"

He smiled. "Yes, ma'am."

She turned to the drawings. "We're in the demolition phase of this project. We have to clean up what was damaged in the mine explosion before we can assess structural damage," Molly said.

Parker added. "Each man has been assigned different areas to work, not too far from each other in case you run into trouble."

Molly pointed to the blueprint. "Drake, you'll take the butler's pantry and coat closet on the far side of the main dining room. The walls are cracked and crumbling. We need to get behind the drywall to see if the support beams have been compromised. Your goal today is to clear the walls on the mountainside of the rooms and any other walls showing significant damage."

Parker raised a hand. "I'll take Drake and Grimm to their locations."

Molly glanced toward the other three men. "The rest are with me. You'll find sledgehammers, battery-powered reciprocating saws, gloves and wheelbarrows staged in each of your areas. The power is off, so you'll have to use the headlamps on your safety helmets. The rooms against the mountain don't get much natural light." She handed Drake a helmet with a headlamp. "Thank you all for answering Hank's call. We needed as many hands as we could get for this project, and sometimes, people are hard to come by in small towns."

Anxious to get to work, Drake plunked his helmet on his head and followed Parker through the maze of hallways to the back of the lodge. They hadn't gone far before they had to stop and turn on their headlamps.

Parker continued, explaining what each room was as they passed doorways. He eventually came to a stop in front of a wooden door. "Grimm, this is your assigned area. Judge, yours is the next room. I'll be two doors down. If something doesn't feel right, get the hell out. We don't know exactly how much damage the explosion caused. I'd rather we err on the side of caution. The sooner we see inside the walls, the sooner we can get to work rebuilding."

"Got it." Grimm pulled on a pair of gloves, wrapped his hands around the handle of a sledge-hammer and nodded. "Nothing like a little demoli-tion to work out all your frustrations. Let's do this."

Judge entered the next room and found what he needed to get started. Parker moved on.

Gloves on, Drake grabbed the sledgehammer and went to work knocking big holes in the plaster on the back wall. Piece by piece, he pulled away the plaster and the narrow wooden slats behind it, exposing a couple of feet of the interior beams at a time.

Plaster dust filled the air, making it more and more difficult to see. Judge found face masks in the stack of supplies and pulled one on over his mouth and nose. He'd made it through half the back wall in less than an hour. If he kept up the pace, he'd have that wall done in the next hour. The other walls in the room had only hairline fractures in the plaster. Hopefully, that was a good sign that they hadn't been damaged to the point they needed to be torn down as well.

One thing was certain; they'd have to wait until the dust settled before they could assess the status of the support beams.

The banging on the wall in the next rooms stopped for a moment.

"Can you see anything?" Grimm called out.

"Not much," Drake responded. "My headlamp is reflecting off all the dust particles."

"Same," Grimm came to stand in the doorway, wearing a mask over his mouth and nose.

"Let the dust settle for a few minutes," Parker called out.

"Have you had a chance to find a place to live?" Grimm asked.

Drake shook his head, his light swinging right then left, bouncing off the dust in the air. "I just got to town and came straight here."

"I think there's room at Mrs. Dottie Kinner's bed and breakfast where I'm staying. You can follow me there after work and ask her yourself if she's got another room available."

"Thanks." Drake glanced across the room. "I think I can see the wall again."

Grimm nodded. "Going back to my wall."

Moments later, the men were slamming their heavy sledgehammers into yet more plaster.

Drake worked on the next four feet of wall, knocking out sheetrock. He grabbed hold of a portion of the drywall and pulled hard. A large portion fell away, exposing a gap between studs that was three feet wide.

Had there been a door there at one time? He removed the rest of the plaster down to the floor and had to wait for the dust to settle in order to see the beams, much less if anything lay beyond the beams.

As the dust slowly settled, Drake's headlamp beam cut through the remaining particles to a room beyond the wall. It wasn't more than six feet by six feet square and had been carved out of the rock wall of the mountain.

He stepped between the beams into the stone-walled room. Several wooden crates littered the floor, along with a pile of what appeared to be clothing. He crossed to the crates and found them to be full of bottles of some kind of liquid. None of the bottles were labeled.

Drake suspected the bottles were moonshine and that the stash was left over from the Prohibition Era. He turned the beam of his headlamp to the pile of clothes on the floor. The cloth had a floral pattern of faded pink and yellow. Perhaps it had once been a curtain or a woman's dress.

As he neared the pile, he noticed a shoe and something that appeared to be a pole or thick stick lying beside it.

His pulse picked up, his empty belly roiling. He leaned over the pile of clothes and the shoe and froze.

The stick wasn't a stick at all. It was a bone. On the other side of it was another bone just like it.

With the handle of his sledgehammer, he moved the crate beside the pile of cloth and gasped.

On the other side of the crate, lying against the cold stone floor, lay a skull covered in a dry mummified layer of skin with a few long, thin strands of hair clinging to it in scattered patches.

"Parker," Drake called out.

When the hammering continued, Drake cleared his throat and yelled. "Parker!"

All hammering ceased.

"That you, Drake?" Parker answered.

With his gaze on what he now had determined was a complete skeleton covered in a woman's dress, Drake said, "You need to come see this."

ABOUT THE AUTHOR

ELLE JAMES also writing as MYLA JACKSON is a *New York Times* and *USA Today* Bestselling author of books including cowboys, intrigues and paranormal adventures that keep her readers on the edges of their seats. When she's not at her computer, she's traveling, snow skiing, boating, or riding her ATV, dreaming up new stories. Learn more about Elle James at www.ellejames.com

Website | Facebook | Twitter | GoodReads | Newsletter | BookBub | Amazon

Or visit her alter ego Myla Jackson at mylajackson.com
Website | Facebook | Twitter | Newsletter

Follow Me!
www.ellejames.com
ellejamesauthor@gmail.com

ALSO BY ELLE JAMES

Shadow Assassin

Delta Force Strong

Brotherhood Protectors Yellowstone

Grimm (#7)

Murdock (#8)

Utah (#9)

Judge (#10)

The Outriders

Homicide at Whiskey Gulch (#1)

Hideout at Whiskey Gulch (#2)

Held Hostage at Whiskey Gulch (#3)

Setup at Whiskey Gulch (#4)

Missing Witness at Whiskey Gulch (#5)

Cowboy Justice at Whiskey Gulch (#6)

Hellfire Series

Hellfire, Texas (#1)

Justice Burning (#2)

Smoldering Desire (#3)

Hellfire in High Heels (#4)

Playing With Fire (#5)

Up in Flames (#6)

Total Meltdown (#7)

Declan's Defenders

Marine Force Recon (#1)

Show of Force (#2)

SEAL's Seduction (#6)

SEAL'S Defiance (#7)

SEAL's Deception (#8)

SEAL's Deliverance (#9)

SEAL's Ultimate Challenge (#10)

Texas Billionaire Club

Tarzan & Janine (#1)

Something To Talk About (#2)

Who's Your Daddy (#3)

Love & War (#4)

Billionaire Online Dating Service

The Billionaire Husband Test (#1)

The Billionaire Cinderella Test (#2)

The Billionaire Bride Test (#3)

The Billionaire Daddy Test (#4)

The Billionaire Matchmaker Test (#5)

The Billionaire Glitch Date (#6)

The Billionaire Perfect Date (#7) coming soon

The Billionaire Replacement Date (#8) coming soon

The Billionaire Wedding Date (#9) coming soon

Ballistic Cowboy

Hot Combat (#1)

Hot Target (#2)

Hot Zone (#3)

Hot Velocity (#4)

Cajun Magic Mystery Series

Voodoo on the Bayou (#1)

Voodoo for Two (#2)

Deja Voodoo (#3)

Cajun Magic Mysteries Books 1-3

SEAL Of My Own

Navy SEAL Survival

Navy SEAL Captive

Navy SEAL To Die For

Navy SEAL Six Pack

Devil's Shroud Series

Deadly Reckoning (#1)

Deadly Engagement (#2)

Deadly Liaisons (#3)

Deadly Allure (#4)

Deadly Obsession (#5)

Deadly Fall (#6)

Covert Cowboys Inc Series

Triggered (#1)

Nick of Time

Alaskan Fantasy

Boys Behaving Badly Anthologies

Rogues (#1)

Blue Collar (#2)

Pirates (#3)

Stranded (#4)

First Responder (#5)

Blown Away

Warrior's Conquest

Enslaved by the Viking Short Story

Conquests

Smokin' Hot Firemen

Protecting the Colton Bride

Protecting the Colton Bride & Colton's Cowboy Code

Heir to Murder

Secret Service Rescue

High Octane Heroes

Haunted

Engaged with the Boss

Cowboy Brigade

Time Raiders: The Whisper

Bundle of Trouble

Killer Body

Operation XOXO

An Unexpected Clue

Baby Bling

Under Suspicion, With Child

Texas-Size Secrets

Cowboy Sanctuary

Lakota Baby

Dakota Meltdown

Beneath the Texas Moon

Made in the USA
Monee, IL
29 October 2024

68908461R00157